PYTHIA

DANIEL SPITERI, SR.

ISBN: 978-912680-41-2 (paperback)
ISBN: 978-1-912680-40-5 (ebook)

Printed in the United States of America

Kingdom International Publishing
www.kingdominternationalpublishing.com
Camarillo, CA
Email: kipbooks@zohomail.com

Library of Congress Control Number:
2021912822

Cover Design by 100Covers.com
Interior Design by FormattedBooks.com

REVIEWS OF *"PYTHIA"*

Pythia ignites smart conversations about a number of important societal topics including gender equality, religion, abortion, and more. Spiteri has done well to create a world mirroring the never-ending issues we have in today's world. This futuristic narrative offers thoughts and concerns about the state of our own time, creating a dystopian atmosphere with a strong purpose and foundation.

Pythia's story asks, "What if?" It has interesting characters, a complex futuristic world, and a platter of themes that book clubs could gather together for lively discussions. For the past thousand years, men took the dominant role in world history creating rules for everything and everyone, especially women. Spiteri reverses the roles, turning them into an alternate future where women rule over men with an iron hand. Fortunately for us, Spiteri provides female characters like Preeta to help us see that not all the women here look down on men as second-class citizens, giving us hope that gender equality, even in the wildest circumstances, can be possible.

Independent Book Review

10.0 out of 10.0 stars

Full of twists and turns, heart-pounding rivalry, excitement and battles, the main character, Simon Peter fights and regains love that he never thought possible. This is an imaginative, creative, and interesting adult novel from an author that reaches deep into the human psyche, bringing forth incentive to not only continue reading his book, but gives a subtle call to get back to God's ways, since proving in this dystopian realm that man left to himself, or in this case, **her**self, only brings complete destruction and chaos upon all that is good and pleasurable. The novel leaves one remembering that to not follow God's natural order of things and people, brings only despair in propagating perverse evil.

Well-done, I would look for more from this author.

—CBM Christian Book Review

Sometimes a book draws in the reader by the action and characters we feel we know personally by the end. This is what Pythia did for me. I truly hope there are sequels to this too-short novel, because I want to learn more about these characters who became very real on the pages. This gem of a page turner held my interest and definitely left me wanting more! I didn't want to stop reading it once I started it.

—Dr. Matthew Agnew
Lead Pastor, Camarillo Christian Church

This book has elements of the movie *Gladiator* and *The Hunger Games* as it sheds light on current hot button topics to get us thinking deeper about our values and Christianity as a reflection of reality.

—Fr. Steve Kim
St. Lucy Catholic Parish,
Campbell, CA

I want to thank J.K Rowling for encouraging me to write this book, to Stephen King for giving me the core ideas explored in this book, to George R. R. Martin for introducing me to my agent, to Amy Tan for helping me discover mother/daughter relationships expressed in this book, to Ayaan Hirsi Ali for editing this book, and to Haruki Murakami for translating my book into Japanese and helping me introduce it into the Japanese market.*

*This ENTIRE BOOK is a work of fiction. All names are the products of the author's imagination. Any resemblance to actual persons, living or dead, is purely coincidental.

This book is dedicated to you, who are compelled to read this book. May you experience vicariously the thrills and dangers of adventure.

PART
ONE

1

The sun shone like it always did, on this day like any other. The sun shines indifferently on mundane days and extraordinary days alike. You might say that this day, as seemingly banal as yesterday, was the beginning of something of historical import like the American Revolution, the birth of Jesus of Nazareth, the tearing down of the Berlin Wall, the invention of the printing press, or the perfection of human cloning, to select a few in a series of many.

Simon Peter (ever since the cloning, all men just had two first names) looked down at the cat. He had always liked cats, although he'd be hard-pressed to give a good reason if you asked him why. Perhaps it was the purring and the meowing—like little motors on a fluffy ball of fur—that drew him to them. Cats provided just a bit of escape from the harshness and drudgery of life. Or perhaps it was the freedom that they exhibited. You cannot herd a cat. And Simon Peter respected and acknowledged the freedom of cats because he was not free. The only freedom he ever experienced was freedom of thought. And in that sense, he felt freer than any educated mistress, because concomitant with education is indoctrination—forced to groupthink, forced to show everyone that you belong in the club. But Simon Peter's very existence—his survival—was an act of rebellion and gave him a sense of freedom. He petted the cat, and tried to hold it to him, but it scurried away.

He sat on an old wooden bench in an enclosure, a cage really, that adjoined the ring. From there, he could see through the bars. Two men were fighting. He knew them both. He had trained with them in the gymnasium, as it was called. Now they were in the coliseum, or as the men preferred to call it, the ring. The coliseum stank of blood and rot, bleach and dirt, sweat, voided bowels and metal. The stands held some 40,000 seats and they were filled with the all-female audience.

To one side of Simon Peter's cage was John John, awaiting his match in another cage. He was the largest fighter in the gymnasium, and as such one of the most revered. John John stood inside his cage with his left foot propped up on a bench and his hands on the bars, looking earnestly at the fight. Without taking his eyes off the fighting men, he said to Simon Peter, "Thanks for leading us in prayer this morning. Takes the edge out of life."

Simon Peter did not respond.

John John continued, "We need that, you know. Hope. Being reminded that God loves us. At least someone loves us."

"Not all the men appreciate my prayers," replied Simon.

"That's true. You can lead a horse to water, but you can't make them drink. But even the men who don't follow Christ respect you."

Out in the arena, Ben Sam and John Ralph were anything but disinterested. One man would live, the other die. That immediacy made for intense concentration and a rush of adrenaline. Physically, the two men were evenly matched, and had about the same years of training. Their win/loss record was about equal, too, but nobody kept track of such things. The gladiators knew that the next match was the only one that mattered. And the fans had no reason to keep track; for them, men were just one step above robots.

Ben Sam wore a breastplate and metal helmet like that of a secutor with only two small eye holes, carried a small shield and used a short sword as his offensive weapon, while John Ralph was lightly armored with no breastplate and no helmet, but a greave, a metal arm guard and a shoulder guard on his dominant sword arm. He, too, carried a small shield.

Ben Sam stalked John Ralph, pivoted toward him and steel clanged on steel. Once, twice, three times. A step back. A jab. They were testing each other, sizing each other up. *How fast is my opponent? How are his reflexes? What is his weakness?* These were the thoughts that ran through both their minds. Their swords rang out together, and gleamed brightly in the sunlight, so much so that, once or twice, some members of the audience would lose sight of the fighters. Musicians soundtracked the action with woodwinds, playing lightly and staccato.

John Ralph backed away and danced to Ben Sam's left side. He was obviously much more agile than his opponent; after all, he was not burdened by heavy metal armor like his adversary. He slashed at Ben Sam's back, a vital area not protected by armor, but the only thing he cut was the air. Ben Sam turned to face John Ralph, shield between them, and thrust at his rival's heart, but John Ralph blocked it with his shield. Ben Sam moved forward, shield up, sword jabbing quickly at the head, the chest, the chest again, the head, slash across from left to right, slash again, jab, jab, slash.

John Ralph was content to play this game. He obliged by moving backward. *If I can possibly tire him out*, he thought. Ben Sam exposed his dominant right side while his sword arm lashed out. John Ralph saw the opportunity and hacked at his opponent's legs, but his reach was too short. The other fighter did the same, just to show that he could be just as agile even weighted down with armor. He wanted his adversary to watch his lower body, too. Ben Sam made contact, but only a clang, while John Ralph hopped lightly and danced even further to his opponent's left.

Shields between them, in a sort of stalemate alignment, Ben Sam had to swivel to his left, too, but this was a more cumbersome challenge for him.

"Fight. Fight," some of the women screamed.

John Ralph looked at the crowd, smiled and winked. A vastly important part of being a gladiator was entertaining your audience. After all, even after a loss, the all-female audience may spare you if they enjoyed your banter, your antics, or if you were visually pleasing to them.

But John Ralph could not spend too much time on showmanship; he had a fight to attend to. And any misstep in this dance meant death.

After more dancing, more parrying, more dodging, more feinting, John Ralph began raining steel. But his competitor met every swipe with the steel of his blade or the metal of his shield. The ringing clash of steel on steel aroused the crowd, and the heart-pounding music intensified. John Ralph was driving into his challenger, but he was being checked each time. Still, the advance continued. John Ralph stepped lightly, never taking his eyes off his foe. He was clearly quicker than Ben Sam, but the other man was well protected. John Ralph lunged, striking only a spark.

Some in the audience demanded their cups be filled. "More wine. More wine," they called to their male servants, while others watched the dance of death intently as if there was nothing else in the world. John Ralph's fans seemed to be the former, while Ben Sam's fans were the latter. The word fans comes from the word fanatics, and it was obvious to see the fanaticism, the fervor of this crowd. The shrieks, the demands to fight and speed up the action were so clear you could almost taste it. You could definitely smell it in the air. It was palpable.

The women's demands for more action only revealed their lack of experience in fighting. For the men in the center of the arena, the action was of vital importance. Did they live to win the purse, which was usually quite a sum? Did they live to please another woman? Did they live to eat another sumptuous victory feast? Did they buy their freedom, at least their freedom from fighting? Or would they be carried off like an unwanted heap of trash?

Simon Peter often thought how he wound up here, a gladiator. A man had only a few occupations from which to choose. He could be a "maker," a word used for both inventors and even mere carpenters. Women could perform these tasks, too, of course, but the women needed some men for this if they wanted to live in comfort and if they wanted to make the world a better place—for themselves.

He could be a soldier. He could be "comfort"— subsumed in that nomenclature was a man used for emotional comfort, or simply for sex. But Simon Peter was a gladiator.

Like almost all men, he had only a rudimentary education, and he did not have the intrinsic talent to be a maker. By dint of his rebellious and impulsive nature, he could never be a soldier. That left this, sitting in what amounted to a cage and waiting to fight his friends—if gladiators could have true friends. He never wanted to fight, but like most prize fighters of the 20th and 21st centuries, he came from the lowest caste. People like him had few choices—from the Irish, to the Italians, to the Blacks, Browns and now, in the year 131OW, simply, men.

John Ralph intensified his attack and, for the first time ever, used his shield as an offensive weapon. He pushed against Ben Sam with all his strength. Ben Sam was clearly the stronger of the two, but the weight of shield and armor and sword will weaken even the most brawny of men. John Ralph pressed forward with shield and sword; Ben Sam defended, but clumsily, and the blade met its mark, catching Ben Sam's shoulder and creating a bright red streak as the razor-sharp blade bit into flesh.

The first wound had a great psychological impact on both fighters. The slasher emboldened, the lacerated disheartened. This more often than not had more of an impact on the outcome of a fight than the physical wound itself. John Ralph hacked again. And again. And then again. Again. Again. And his lurching hacks and prods were met with faint crunching sounds that women in the first few rows could hear.

John Ralph felt the end was near. Glory would be his. The admiration of the women would be his. But as soon as he imagined the win, Ben Sam threw an arching hack that met his metal arm guard with a crunch. The blow cracked open his arm guard, which sheared in half and hung by its leather straps.

John Ralph backed away out of harm's reach. He reverted back to his dance of jabs and slashes, holding up his shield for protection. Ben Sam was able to parry, but he was getting slower and slower. John Ralph once again took advantage of Ben Sam's weakness. He made overarching hacking motions with his sword, abandoning all that he had learned in his training. All, that is, except for "If you see blood, go for blood." Many of these blows met with metal, adding to the song of steel on steel. The musicians sensed, too, the end was near and sounded their climatic finale of trumpets and horns.

John Ralph seemed to be getting stronger, faster; he found his second wind. He charged, leading with the edge of his shield, which caught his enemy's helmet. The shield slid down the helmet and met the flesh of Ben Sam's naked neck while the helmet slid up just enough that the slits no longer lined up with Ben Sam's eyes. Ben Sam reeled back off his back foot and lost his balance, staggered and fell. They say the bigger they are, the harder they fall and as long as they do not fall on you, all the better.

John Ralph threw down his shield and with both hands placed the tip of his sword on his vanquished adversary's neck. He looked up at the Supreme Leader and when she gave the thumbs down, he plunged his blade deep into the neck of his enemy.

All was still in the ring. The audience's shrieks and howls subsided, waiting for the best part of the competition—the honoring of the Supreme Leader. John Ralph raised his arms in the air in triumph, his right hand still holding the blade, with his arm guard still dangling by its straps. He was dehydrated and he could smell his own urine, having passed water from fear before the fight, which was normal for men in battle. He approached the Supreme Leader, bowed and honored her by standing straight and stiff, holding out both arms to his side as if to make the letter "M," the salute of Pythia, and roared, "Matriarchy Forever," the slogan of the realm. The crowd cheered.

2

As the loser was unceremoniously (and de-gradingly) dragged out of the ring like the carcass of a rabid dog, Simon Peter dropped to his knees in the rear of the cage so as not to be seen, and prayed.

He had learned of this thing called prayer while in grade school. The gladiators were an important part of society. They provided entertainment and escape, but more than that, they helped solidify the power of the state. As such, they enjoyed a bit of so-called freedom. As long as they trained, as long as they fought, they were not watched as closely as the house slaves. Because of this, one of Simon Peter's trainers was able to introduce him to the Christian faith. In that regard, he was lucky. And at every opportunity that he could get, Simon passed on the faith to any gladiator who would listen. This was all done in secret; the women-folk would not abide the teachings of Christianity.

After the cloning, women discovered that they could allow men to be educated up to a point. After all, the women-run government had a monopoly on education. So schools and universities, for all intents and purposes, were more indoctrination than education. Just as Christian schools (before the Clone Wars when they were allowed to exist) did not teach students to challenge the teachings of Jesus Christ, and just like military schools did not teach students to challenge their superior officers, so these government-run schools did not teach anything contrary to the tenets of the government; that is, the superiority of women over men. And the women found the men more pleasant, more civilized, after being allowed this education. Some men were even allowed higher education. As long as the majority could overwhelm the minority, the status quo was maintained. Militarily, women outnumbered men, so as long as men could be watched, as long as men could be monitored, they could concomitantly be controlled.

Simon Peter recalled learning about the past religions of the world. He was taught by his teachers and his textbooks (and all media) that all religions were "the opiate of the masses," nothing more than quaint superstition. After the cloning, all religion had been banned. The incongruously named Department of Religion was tasked with rooting out all religious practitioners and meting out proper consequences. This usually meant death or imprisonment for men, a steep fine and "re-education" classes for women.

The Department of Religion employed thousands of women across the country. They were responsible for the "management" of all religions; they focused, though, on Christianity. After all, you cannot allow the notion that God made each of us and that we are made in the image of God and all of us are equal under God, while simultaneously subjugating a portion of your population. And what was more, Christianity, like all the other religions, made it difficult for the state to prevent alternate sources of authority. To the state, all authority should rest with the state.

But Simon Peter did not see it that way. Even though his teachers scoffed at the idea, he saw Christianity as a reflection of reality. He saw that when Old Europe adopted Christianity, its scientific discoveries blossomed. He might not have been the most educated man, but he saw through the propaganda—he was able to read between the lines.

Because of what he had learned from one of his trainers, he knew that before Christianity, all the religions of the world (save Judaism, which, thankfully, gave rise to Christianity) had many, many gods. You had the god of wine, the god of war, the god of your enemies, even the god of water. You had a plethora of gods. This instilled within the people the idea that the universe, that our world, was chaotic. But the Jews came up with the idea of one God, creator of everything, so that there was a universal right and wrong. This invariably led to a desire, for the first time in human history, to try to discover the work of God—to find out how God made the world, how God made the universe. Christianity led to the scientific method and, ultimately, the scientific revolution and modernity and progress and personal freedom that the world had never seen before. And not only that, the realization that there was only one true God led people to the realization that God created us all, that we have certain inalienable God-given rights. In short, it gave rise to personal freedom, and would have led to the end of slavery, genocide and cloning if it had not been stunted by the humanists and the power of the state.

And so Simon Peter prayed. He asked God to make him a servant of peace. He saw the contradiction between his avocation and his desire to be a man of God, but what could he do? He was essentially powerless to determine his own destiny. He prayed to end this barbaric practice of gladiators fighting to the death but, for good measure, he also prayed to be the victor in his fight.

After Ben Sam was disgracefully pulled from the arena floor and out of sight of the spectators, but before the guards could collect Simon for his fight, he stood up so that his praying would go unnoticed by the guards. The guards opened the door to his cage and handed him his martial outfit. From his shoulder all the way down his right arm, he was outfitted with a guard made of chain mail. And when he was clad in his mail, he stood a little bit straighter. He seemed a little bit taller, even to himself.

He was not a short man, but not one you might call tall, either. Ethnic diversity was appreciated in Simon Peter's day, but that recognition, that privilege, was reserved only for women-folk so that Simon Peter was not in touch with his ethnic background. He was unaware of his roots and, just as a tree needs roots to grow, so does a man. Frost does not touch deep roots and the powers that be knew this all too well. It was easier to manipulate people who did not know from where they came. Divide and conquer is one of the oldest tricks in the book, used by governments for centuries. The authorities realized long ago that it was difficult to achieve the social disintegration needed to gain control by promoting class division alone. Thus they employed every trick in the book; so-called "race", religion, gender, you name it. It worked. The only remaining division was those who professed allegiance to the world order versus those who opposed it. Racial harmony is possible, but only in free societies where all are treated equally by the government. Anything short of that is meant to first divide, then enslave us all. And this was the epoch that Simon Peter found himself living in. He was not truly cut out for gladiator competition, but, given the limited number of choices for men, this was his best option. He had often thought, if he had been lucky enough to have been born a woman (or if people were measured by competence in a truly egalitarian society), that he would have been a poet or maybe even a politician.

But life was what it was, and he focused once again on his armor. In his left hand, he held a short sword with a hilt and guard. In his dominant right hand, he used a flail, a small metal handle attached to a metal chain at the end of which was a metal ball with small knobs or flanges. This was believed to be a powerful medieval weapon by the powers that be, but in actuality, the flail was rarely used in medieval times or at any time in history, really. And there is no evidence it was ever used by gladiators in the Roman Colosseum. Nevertheless, the female leaders thought it was a brutal and effective weapon.

Simon Peter knew otherwise. He was well aware that he would be telegraphing his strikes using the flail. He also knew that if he missed, the ball might bounce back and hit him. No wonder they had the expression "to flail about." And since the organizers of the gladiator games thought this flail to be such a superior weapon, Simon had no shield. Nor did he have a helmet.

Before he was let out of his cage, John John called to Simon Peter in a voice just loud enough for him to hear, yet not within earshot of the guards. "Put on the full armor of God, so that you can take your stand against the devil's schemes. For our struggle is not against flesh and blood, but against the rulers, against the authorities, against the powers of this dark world."

This distracted Simon Peter, but he remained steadfast. He had a job to do.

When he was brought out to the center of the arena, he saw his opponent. He knew him. They had trained at the Bellona Gladiator School together. His name was Adam Levi, though Simon Peter did not know him by name. Simon remembered Adam as a conscientious and hard-working student who always took his drills seriously and who seemed to relish his sparring matches. They had never exchanged words, but one day while Simon was on his knees praying, Adam had walked by and scoffed, "So primitive. You sing the praises of God, but you don't see scientists singing the praises of gravity. Yet gravity exists." Adam wore a breastplate, and a greave on each leg, and carried a long spear and a large wooden shield. Like Simon, he wore no helmet.

When Simon saw the spear and shield, he thought, *I've got to get inside. Gotta neutralize that spear.*

Adam took one look at Simon and taunted, "I hope your God is a merciful one. You're going to meet Her soon enough."

Why did they match up a long spear with a flail and short knife? Such a mismatch. I will have to use my flail as a sort-of shield to keep him at bay while I try to get inside with my knife, Simon thought. *I don't think this will be a fight to the death. After all, they have spent a lot of money on us. A lot of money and womanpower has gone into our training. We are entertainers, really. We are more useful to the cause alive than dead. They only kill the Undesirables and the ones they find in the No-Go Zones.* At least that was what he told himself, for one fleeting moment.

That was the last thought he had the luxury of entertaining before Adam rushed toward him, thrusting his spear. Simon dodged to the inside and flung his flail, which Adam's shield blocked easily. But Simon made another swing. And another. And another. Wood chips flew off the shield from the repeated blows.

Simon swung high. Simon swung low. Simon came in at all angles, yet Adam was able to block every blow. *That shield is just too damn big,* thought Simon. He feinted with his knife hand, then swung the flail again. But the shield was too large; Adam could almost set it on the ground and stand behind it. And this time a chunk of wood came spiraling off the shield, but the flail bounced back and hit Simon on the shoulder. If it were not for his chain mail, this might have incapacitated his right arm entirely. He would have been reduced to fighting one-handed. He thought, *Why am I given a flail of all weapons? I would prefer a shield to this undependable weapon.*

But there was no time for thought. Adam capitalized on Simon's loss of rhythm and feinted with the point of his spear, then pulled it back and slashed at Simon's face. He bent backward quickly like a cat. Adam thrust again, this time aiming for Simon's unprotected chest. *A shield*, Simon thought again as he flung his flail around in a sort of figure-eight to act like a shield or screen, much like a nunchaku.

It seemed to be working; it seemed to confuse Adam, who had never seen a flail used in that manner. He continued jutting with his spear, sending its point straight into Simon's ribs. Simon flicked away the end of the spear almost insultingly with his whirlwind flail.

He cannot keep this up for much longer. Surely he will tire soon. He must. That flail will tire his arm and then I will reach my mark with my spear. This was Adam's strategy. Good fighters (the ones who survive) often changed their strategies mid-fight. To stick to the same game plan was suicide. New facts, new game.

But Simon got lucky. His flail caught the end of the spear in just the perfect manner such that the spiked ball and chain snapped the metal head off. The head of the spear spun like a pinwheel and landed on the dirt. Now Simon started raining blows on his opponent's shield with relentless repetition. Over and over he landed on the shield. Adam could do nothing but block and hope that Simon would fatigue. But Simon would not tire; at least not yet.

Wooden splinters flew. The shield cracked down the middle. Simon persisted, taking advantage of Adam's vulnerability. The shield was reduced to kindling. It shattered, one piece careening through the air, while another clung stubbornly to his arm, held with leather straps. Adam tried to free himself from this useless appendage. His shield was now his enemy.

Simon was ready to end this battle. He flung his weapon into Adam's breastplate. The force of the blow sent the other man reeling backwards. Had it not been for the armor, half of his ribs would have been shattered. But as it was, Simon's weapon was stuck in his enemy's breastplate. He tried to pull it free, but Adam spun around.

The women were cheering wildly.

The two men stood facing each other, each trying to catch his breath and figure out his next stratagem. Adam still had the shaft of his spear, so he used it as a staff, holding it in two hands due to its length and bulk. He began pressing an offensive attack against Simon. He still had the reach advantage since Simon only had his short knife. Left strike, right strike, backlash, swinging, always attacking, moving in, sliding, striking, stepping, striking, faster, faster, faster. Simon was forced backward, slipped on the broken shield on the ground and fell with a thud. The impact made him grunt and lose his knife, which slid along the dirt ground only a few feet away, yet far enough to be useless. Now Simon had no weapon, no protection and was clearly in a vulnerable position.

"Where is your God now?" taunted Adam, as he turned his spear around to employ its blunt handle. He began beating Simon about the head, landing blow after authoritative blow. Hard and fast came the wallops. As the shaft came crashing down on him, Simon saw the spearhead. *One chance,* he thought. He scurried to the double-edged blade, grabbed it by what little wooden handle was left while his adversary was striking his back, and swung about in a blind slash at Adam.

With sheer blind luck, he met his mark. The spear cut Adam's hand, and the pain of the laceration sent him recoiling backward. Simon leaped up and, panther-like, knocked Adam to the ground, touching the spearhead's point to his vanquished adversary's neck. He looked up at the Supreme Leader as she gave the thumbs down, yet he dropped the spear point to the ground. *For our struggle is not against flesh and blood, but against the rulers...* He made the sign of the cross and stood up, leaving his opponent lying in the dirt.

Simon Peter did not look at the Supreme Leader. Simon Peter did not raise his hands in victory. Simon Peter did not make the obligatory salute of the times. Simon Peter did not yell, "Matriarchy Forever." He simply walked out of the arena in disgust.

The audience was stunned. That is, the women were stunned. The male slaves were, probably for the first time in their lives, equally astonished, yet full of pride. *Is this pride?* many thought. *Is this how it feels to feel dignity?* They could not tell; they had never felt like this before. Outwardly, the men tried to hide their smiles, tried to erase the gleam in their eyes; but inwardly...oh, inwardly...what a show of respect. Not respect for the maternalist society in which they lived, not respect for the oppression and lack of choices they had to live under, not respect for being used like so much meat, but *self*-respect.

The women in the audience looked to their Supreme Leader to see how she would react. To see how *they* would react; after all, this had never happened before. The Supreme Leader, Fidelity Flake, simply stood up from her seat and left the coliseum with her retinue in tow. But Fidelity's daughter Preeta did not walk out with her mother. The remaining women in Fidelity Flake's entourage began to boo and throw things into the arena. But Preeta did not. The other women screamed and yelled epithets. But Fidelity's daughter did not. Preeta merely looked on, and then, after some time standing there looking at the desolation of the arena, she walked out of the coliseum alone.

When the commoners observed the behavior of the women in Fidelity's court, they understood their cue. They, too, began to boo and throw their drinks and food into the arena.

3

Simon Peter's room was relatively lavish, complete with a bed and a full bathroom and all the comforts he would need. He was even allowed books. There was no kitchen, though he was allowed a small refrigerator, because meals were carefully prepared for the gladiators, with nutrition being of paramount importance. There was even a large picture window overlooking the grounds and the countryside beyond, and since his suite was on the top floor, he even had a skylight.

For the most part, gladiators were treated well; they were an important part of the social order and helped keep the oppressive matriarchy alive. Nice environs to be sure, but a prison cell nonetheless because he was not allowed his freedom. He was told when to wake up in the morning, he was told when to eat, what to do during the day, and when to retire at night. He was not free to leave the gymnasium nor did he choose this life. He was a captive of the matriarchy. When a man can no longer choose, he is not a man.

As Simon Peter walked out of his shower, Preeta entered his room. As the daughter of the Supreme Leader, she was treated concomitantly like a princess and a prime minister. She had wisdom beyond her twenty-three years and she held the respect of the people.

She wore a white sleeveless pullover dress with a plunging V neckline. She had a purple wrap, edged in gold satin, draped over her left shoulder. She wore platinum armbands on both her arms. "Don't dress on account of me," she began. Simon was taken aback by this and felt self-conscious and vulnerable.

He draped his towel around himself and stammered something about getting dressed. It was largely inaudible, but she got the gist.

"I don't think I made myself clear: Don't dress on account of me," she repeated. Simon wrapped the towel around himself tighter and knotted it. Preeta approached, pressed herself against him and said, "You fought very boldly."

"Thank you," he said, as he tried to back away.

Preeta continued to press herself closely to Simon until they were up against a wall. Simon looked out the window and she repeated, "You fought very boldly," as she caressed his chest.

"That is my job," he said abruptly. "I hope the delegation found it entertaining."

"Well, I don't know about the delegation," she giggled breathily, "but I most certainly was enthralled."

"Why didn't you kill the boy?" she cooed, as she kissed his lips, neck and face softly.

Simon was taken aback by the kiss and did not reciprocate. "Not a boy, ma'am. A man. He is a man."

"I like that answer," she said while continuing to kiss him. "But why didn't you kill…the man?"

He feared explaining his Christian faith and his belief that God made all of us in His image. He thought explaining the sanctity of life—especially the life of a mere man—too much for her to comprehend. She would just laugh at him; scoff at his belief in this ancient tradition that was lost after the Clone Wars. "Difficult to explain, ma'am," he said, still looking coldly out the window. He thought that if he could just mentally transport himself outside of the room, then maybe this seduction wouldn't be so bad. Maybe if he could really fix his thoughts on the outside, that this would not be happening at all. What was a man to do?

She replied, in a very coy fashion, "Well, I guess you have a little secret that you're keeping from me." She reached underneath his towel and felt his manhood. She grinned. "Or maybe it's not so little."

He remained frozen, still looking out the window, not at her.

She changed tactics a bit. "Why are you playing so hard to get?"

"I'm sorry, ma'am, this doesn't seem right. I am a lowly gladiator. You are in the head of government and the Supreme Leader's daughter."

"Well, my young man, first of all, no more 'ma'am'—and that's an order." She smiled as she grabbed his backside and continued lightly kissing him. "And what is so wrong about it?"

"What would your mother say?"

"I don't see my mother here."

"She will find out just the same. She is very powerful, and she would be against you being with a man like me."

"Yes, a man like you. Or any man, for that matter. But I can tell her we are going to visit the precincts and that I need you on my bodyguard detail. Then you and I could go to the No-Go Zone and nobody would ever think to look for us there."

"Yes, ma'am. Sorry Preeta," he corrected himself. "Yes, Preeta, that's true, but we cannot go to the No-Go Zone. You know as well as I that it is desolate and radioactive. It is no place for life."

"Oh, that is sooo cute. You know you can't believe everything they teach you in school." She took a half-step back from Simon, and pulled off her dress and wrap so that the only thing she wore were her armbands. "Look at me," she demanded. "Look at me."

He looked at her. He wanted her. Seeing her standing there like that was sort-of incongruous in his mind. She was the powerful sex, the dominant sex, yet she looked so vulnerable and he felt badly that he was not reciprocating her advances. His demeanor softened and he said, "I am using all my strength…"

"Use all your strength in the arena, use half your strength with me," she retorted.

He smiled.

"Simon, I got a smile out of you. That gives me hope, Simon." She picked up her clothes and dressed herself. She gave him a peck on the cheek and walked to the door, where she turned around and said, "I realize I can just have you anytime I wish, but I want you to want me, Simon. Maybe I can prove myself to you." She left the room.

Strange, he thought. *She could have me anytime she wanted. Why did she try to seduce me like that? Usually women just demand sex; that is their privilege. And what did she mean by "proving herself to me"?*

Simon spent the rest of that day in his room, resting and ruminating over Preeta's advances. He was used to women using men for sex, but it seemed to him that she wanted more. She actually wanted him to want her. She even kissed him, something women did not do with men.

4

The next day, he went out to the yard where the men were allowed to relax and play games and to experience fraternity with each other. They were a close bunch. They experienced a tight bond and a close brotherhood. After all, they were all thrown into this together. They were fully aware that they were being used for the entertainment of women, much like female beauty pageants centuries before. They understood that they were at once athletes and entertainers, but also satisfied the blood lust of the people. As Fidelity was fond of saying, "Give the people alcohol, marijuana and gladiators and we keep the political power."

Most of the men treated their fellow combatants like brothers. They cared for them when they were sick. They lent or outright gave their clothes to their fellow men. They consoled each other in difficult times. Even though they knew in the back of their minds that they might be fighting each other soon, they supported each other. Having said that, there were some men, a minority, who kept to themselves. They were not anti-social or antagonistic to the other men in any way; on the contrary, they were the most sensitive ones—the ones who could not bear to harm someone they considered a friend.

It was into this environment that Simon entered. Some men were sunbathing while drinking their allotment of wine. Some were playing catch. Some were playing cards, and others were just engaged in discussion.

Preeta was called to the Central Committee Chambers by her mother, Fidelity. On her way to the Chambers, she wondered why her mother would summon her. *There is no Central Committee meeting, no edicts to be proclaimed. Why does she want to meet in the Chambers? It can't be of a personal nature, can it? Does she know? Does she know about my involvement in the liberation? She can't. How could she? I'm just being paranoid. Being involved in any conspiracy, especially one plotting against the government, especially plotting*

against your own mother, is bound to make you paranoid. But just because you are paranoid does not mean you are wrong. You can be paranoid **and** *there can actually be people on to you. Two things can be true at the same time. I am sure of one thing: I cannot be sure of anything. I must meet with her calmly, as if nothing is wrong. Nothing is wrong. I am just meeting with my mother because my mother called for me. That is perfectly normal. But what is the new normal? Even calling Fidelity "mother" is not normal. At least not the way it had been for thousands of years prior to The Cloning. She did not even give birth to me. She did not even get impregnated by any man. I am merely my mother's DNA. I am basically her. Why we continue to say "mother" is beyond me. Maybe "mother-hood" is just another means of power, just another way to own somebody.*

These were the thoughts that flew around in Preeta's head, the thoughts that she had to suppress. She walked into the Central Committee Chamber, which was a huge glass-ceilinged atrium, ornately decorated with authentic Roman sculptures, sepa-rated into two areas. One had senate-type seating with a central rostrum in the front of the room, while the other area was one of many personal quar-ters for the Supreme Leader. There was no gallery. There was no need for one because the public had no right to witness the proceedings of the Central Committee.

How strange, Preeta thought. *How downright schizophrenic is our government. These chambers, mixing the personal chambers with Central Committee Chambers, are indicative of how our government mixes the personal with the political. All throughout history, no matter if we call it slavery, serfdom, democracy, republicanism, communism, socialism, monarchy, theocracy, all of humanity throughout history can be divided into those who want to control other people and those who do not. Those who want power versus those who want to be left alone. Those who want to control how you live, and those who want to simply live and let live.*

It was into this environment that Preeta entered. Her mother was sitting on her couch in her personal chambers. There was no one else in the atrium—no general secretaries, no prime ministers, no council members, not even any bodyguards or entourage. This would be personal.

Simon walked over to the men who were chatting, a group of six or seven men. Among those men was his best friend, John John, who was an oak of a man, someone you would definitely want on your side. And certainly John John was very dedicated to Simon Peter. Even though John John towered over Simon Peter, he looked up to Simon—he admired his leadership skills. As a matter of fact, this was not the first time that Simon Peter had given it to The Woman. This latest incident was only the most recent in a long line of insubordination and noncompliance. But this was the first time he had done so many rebellious things so publicly.

As Simon approached, John John hollered, "Here he comes. The man himself. The legend. The myth. The badass. And the fool who will get himself killed if he is not careful." He winked at his buddies, who looked up to him in almost the same way that he looked up to Simon.

Simon just smiled, looked up to the sky, and deflected, "Nice day today. Nice day indeed."

"What is the matter with you, man? What is with you? Why can't you just conform? I'm surprised you made it this far without Fidelity having your head served to her on a silver platter."

"What did I do? I haven't done anything."

"Come in. Come in," said Fidelity. "Have a seat, honey, and share some fruit and chocolate with me."

Honey? She only calls me honey when I am in trouble or she is trying to get me to do something. Preeta sat next to her mother on the couch, but did not touch the treats.

"Eat something, honey. Some things are better shared."

Preeta took a chocolate-covered strawberry. "Thank you, Mother."

"That's it. That's it. Wonderful day, isn't it? A beautiful day to relax. We have such a nice climate here in Delilah."

"Is that why you called me here, to give me a weather report on our state capitol?"

"Oh, you are so funny. So clever. Can't a mother just want to spend some quality time with her daughter?"

"Yes, yes, that would be nice. I can't remember spending much quality time together."

"Well we can start now. Quality time together is an important thing."

"It's everything," corrected Preeta.

"Ah, look at him, Mr. Innocent," said John John. "You know what you done, you made the sign of the cross yesterday. You know, that Christian thing."

"I've made the sign of the cross before."

"Yeah, yeah, yeah." John John shook his head. "But that was here in the gymnasium before eating a meal, not in front of the whole city of Delilah looking at you, for Sanger's sake. Nobody cares what we do in here as long as we train and fight. There are no cameras here. The government leaves us alone, pretty much. We are important to them. In many ways, we are free, like dogs and cats are free. As long as we perform. And you are damn lucky that you have fighting skills. But there's a limit. And not making the sign of Matriarchy crosses that line. What has gotten into you?"

"You see, you are my clever girl," said Fidelity. "You are my clever girl. How is your social life?"

"My social life? Ummm, it's fine, I guess. I mean, it is the same as it ever was—the usual."

"I hear you tried to seduce the gladiator. You know, the one who refused to do the sign of Matriarchy and other such atrocities."

"Like you said, I made the sign of the cross, not the sign of Matriarchy," said Simon Peter. "God is here for everyone—not just for women, but for men and women equally. Matriarchy is exclusive. Christianity is inclusive."

"And you did not end the man's life. I mean, I'm glad you did not, but you disobeyed Fidelity's thumb of death. I say, for Sanger's sake, what has gotten into you, man?"

"Well, my friend, I can lay the blame at your feet. It was all your fault."

"All...me? Now you are going to have to explain that one to me."

"Before my fight, you called out Ephesians 6, verses 11 and 12. That was the mustard seed that took root in my heart and I could not ignore it."

"Yes," John John agreed, "those are powerful words. 'Take up the shield of faith, with which you can extinguish all the flaming arrows of the evil one. Take the helmet of salvation and the sword of the Spirit...'"

"...which is the word of God," they finished in unison, then laughed.

John John continued, "I'm telling you, you better be careful. And what is up with you not pleasing Preeta Flake? That right there is cause for death."

Surprised, Preeta answered, "Did you hear that through the grapevine?"

"I think 'a little bird told me' is more apropos. I have my ways, I have my spies. I have eyes and ears everywhere. I must protect the state, and me and you."

"I suppose in that order, too."

"Well, word travels fast around here," Simon answered.

"What do you expect, we are a small community and we watch out for each other. Cause for death,

I'm telling you. Or did you forget what happened to Tyrone Frank?"

"I did not forget. Maybe I did it *for* him. And maybe it was because I am not in love with Preeta."

"Listen, darling," chided Fidelity, "I would prefer you stick with our kind. Having said that, you may from time to time indulge in a man's pleasures if that is what suits you, but you must keep in mind your station in life. You are the daughter of the Supreme Leader, in line to become Leader yourself. Remember: 'Wham, blurr—thank you, sir.'"

At that, all the men laughed. *How is love involved? Love has nothing to do with it. It is just your job to provide comfort for women.*

"You are just a man. You need to know your place. You know that I love you; you are like a brother to me. You have to know your place. Just have sexual intercourse with her. Just give her pleasure, achieve orgasms. You can keep your dignity by not ejaculating yourself, and for Sanger's sake, don't kiss her, man."

"Why did you try to seduce him when you could just have him?" Fidelity continued. "Men are a dime a dozen and all for the taking."

"I wanted him to want me, too," Preeta snapped.

The other men laughed. "You kissed her?" one asked.

"Hey, shut the Trump up! You're not fit to kiss this man's feet," John John said in defense of Simon.

"But you said the exact..."

"For Sanger's sake, shut it. I am talking to Simon Peter, who is a credit to our gender and makes us feel proud to be the weaker sex. Men, take leave from us, please, I implore you. I have something personal to say to our beloved Simon Peter."

"You better watch your mouth, girl. Men are dangerous. Men are animals. Masculinity is toxic. They almost ended life on Pythia with their masculinity, their wars, their fighting, their non-cooperative attitude," growled Fidelity.

"Women didn't do much better. We decimated men and much of Earth—I'm sorry, I mean Pythia—during the Clone Wars."

"Better than the alternative."

"Same if you ask me. Now we live in a world largely without men."

Unquestioningly, silently, the men sauntered off. A few of them looked back, but John John waved them off and indicated to them to continue beyond earshot.

John John approached Simon Peter, towering over him and without another word, threw a right cross, fully intending to clock the only man he looked up to. But Simon Peter ducked, dug his shoulders into John John's hips, tackled him and shot at his legs in a double-leg takedown which stunned John John, who thought he had the element of surprise on his side. After Simon Peter got John John on the ground, he playfully slapped John repeatedly in the face.

"Look. You have to please the Central Committee women. Use your sexuality," said John John while Simon was slapping him.

"I want to save myself for the right woman at the right time."

"And we don't need them," continued Fidelity. "They are good for some things, darling, but if their numbers become too great, we women are in danger.

Don't forget that. It is better to keep their numbers small and clone women almost exclusively—except for the few we need for certain things, like sex. And even for that, women are better. Who knows a woman's body better than another woman? I am right, darling. I am right."

"Maybe for you, but I prefer a man."

"Too bad for you, but remember darling, you can have one any time you'd like. Remember that."

"But men can be good for so much more. Given the opportunity, they can invent things, they can protect us. Not all men are toxic, not all masculinity is toxic. A man's natural nature is to protect us from harm. Is that so bad?"

"That is not up to you," John John scoffed.

"I refuse to be used like a piece of meat."

"That is your destiny."

"Nobody should be mistreated because of the shape of their skin."

"Only if they can be controlled," replied Fidelity. "Naturally, men are disposable partners to women rather than protectors of us. Remember it was women who civilized ancient man when they used to roam free."

"'Roam free.' I hate when you make them sound like animals. They are just like us. We can be equals."

John John pivoted his hips forward, maneuvered his leg over Simon's arm and around his head and wrapped that leg around the ankle of his other foot, holding Simon in a triangular choke hold with his feet. "You need to satisfy her. No emotions, just sex."

Simon Peter picked up John John while still in the leg triangle choke hold and body slammed the larger man to the ground.

With a thud, John John's grasp was loosened enough for Simon Peter to regain full guard. Stunned and dazed, John John lay there, staring blankly at the sky until he gained lucidity. He laughed. Simon laughed, too, and pulled John John to his feet.

"Be careful, brother, you might have to give up some skin to keep your skin," said John John.

"You cannot make unequal things equal, try as you might. Men are nothing like us, darling," said Fidelity. "They are nothing like us. And what is more, we can invent things, too. We don't need men for that."

"Yes, but in the old days, men invented automobiles and ships and computers and light. Why, they even sent a man to the moon."

"Why stop at one man, darling? Why not send them all," Fidelity cooed.

"I'm saving myself, John John," said Simon. "Actually saving myself for the woman I will love and the woman who will bear my children. That's right, I mean having offspring naturally, like we were meant to do, not by cloning ourselves, which is so narcissistic."

"You must really hate men deeply to make jokes like that," said Preeta.

"Very virtuous, my friend, very virtuous," said John John.

"Oh darling, it is not so much that I hate men, it is more that I love women," said Fidelity.

"Well, you want to be a man, don't you? To be a real man, you must have virtue; and to be a free man you must choose right from wrong, which, again, means you must have virtue," said Simon Peter.

"For Sanger's sake, you don't have to be anti-man to be pro-woman," said Preeta.

"Yes, to be a man," said John John dreamily, almost to himself. "I would love to be considered a man—I mean a whole man. Not just a body, not just a fighter, but a whole person, not just a disposable trophy for a woman. I so long for my freedom. You don't know how often I think about my freedom. The freedom to express myself as I see fit, the freedom to engage freely with other people, the freedom to go about freely wherever I desire, even just the freedom to think my own thoughts. You talk about virtue; I would settle for freedom."

"Freedom does not make you virtuous; rather, freedom provides you with the opportunity to choose between right and wrong, between doing good versus doing evil. Your choices, then, make you virtuous," said Simon as they walked over to the rest of the men.

"You are so naive. You are so naive. But no matter," said Fidelity. "As you age, you will learn; you will see that I am right and you are wrong. You will change your..."

"No, I will not change my ways. You're the one who is wrong. Your future is no future. We need our counterparts, our yin and yang, we are like a magnet with one pole, only north, no south. We cannot survive like..."

"We are done talking here, my pretty. You may leave. I am your mother, but you must never forget that I am the Supreme Leader. The world needs me. Pythia needs me for stability, for peace. You, young lady, shall not disrupt the peace. If you are seen with that balls again... You are forbidden to see that balls again. Pick another set of balls, they are all the same in the dark. Goodbye."

PART
TWO

L ater that day, Fidelity called a meeting of her closest advisors to discuss this
testosterone-poisoned upstart. Present were
Savy Noir, Secretary of State; Saridian
Ventue, Secretary of War; Colma Caris, Secretary
of the Interior; Perfidia Nagate, Secretary of Media;
and Listras Sumi, Secretary of Loyalty. Preeta, next
in line to become Supreme Leader, was conspicuous
by her absence. Fidelity decided against her daughter attending the meeting; after all, she thought,
if Preeta actually wanted a man to want her, what
would come next? That men were equal? Such her-
esy could not be tolerated.

Fidelity knew the tenuousness of her position. She, like all politicians throughout history, desired most to retain power. If Fidelity had her way, there would be a gendercide and the emergence of Übermensch Womon. *I long for the annihilation of men. If I could rid myself of the weaker sex, I would have gallows built in rows, as many as traffic allowed. Then men would be hanged indiscriminately, and they would remain hanging until they stank, as long as the principles of hygiene permitted. As soon as they had been untied, the next batch would be strung up, and so on down the line, until the last man in the city of Delilah had been exterminated. Other cities would follow suit, precisely in this fashion, until all of Pythia was rid of testosterone-laced men.*

But she did not give voice to her thoughts; wisely, she kept them to herself. She did however tell her staff that she had called the meeting to decide what to do with Simon Peter. She did not have to explain why; they knew the gravity of his offence. Not making the sign of the M, not shouting "Matriarchy Forever," and not saluting the Supreme Leader were intolerable and could easily lead to a degradation of the social order, a breakdown of societal norms, and lawlessness and violence. The powers that be would not stand for such a thing. They all agreed to that.

After Fidelity presented her case, Saridian spoke first. "Clearly an example must be made of him."

All the others except for Savy chimed in with a series of resounding yesses. Saridian said, "We cannot allow the seeds of insurrection to take root and blossom into a full-scale revolution, the fruits of which will be difficult to destroy. Therefore, ladies, to continue my metaphor, we need to nip this in the bud."

Perfidia laughed, "Very flowery words." She winked at Saridian. "Perhaps you should be Secretary of Media."

Colma said, "I think we all agree something should be done, but what? Exactly how should he be punished?"

"Whatever we choose to do, we must make it public," Listras chimed in.

"So good to hear we are all in agreement. I move that he receive a public beating and then a parading through town, with everything published in the media," said Fidelity.

"I second the motion," said Saridian.

"Wait," said Savy, speaking up for the first time. "We have not opened up the motion for discussion. I think we should reconsider. A public beating would not be appropriate here. Simon Peter is, after all, very popular with the male slaves and with many of the common folk, the women I mean. We don't want to turn him into some kind of living martyr."

"What are you proposing?" asked Listras.

"I am proposing that we do nothing. That would show the people the true power of the state. Mercy... mercy, woman, is the true sign of power."

"I think a bullet to the head is faster," Saridian joked.

"You talk like a fool," Savy replied.

Saridian laughed, "How else would you understand me?"

"It is better to keep your mouth shut. That way, people would not know you are a fool. When you open your mouth, you prove it," Savy retorted.

Fidelity intervened. "That is enough. You are acting like men."

"But I was not <u>insulting</u> her," said Savy. "I was merely <u>describing</u> her."

"We shall get back to the subject at hand, and talk about what kind of message we shall send Simon Peter and his ilk, and only about that," Fidelity said.

"Yes," said Savy. "Yes. As I was saying, showing forgiveness is power. We are modern, but we admire the Roman era. That is why we have erected coliseums, that is why we have reinstated gladiator games. The power of the Roman emperor was not the power to punish, but rather the power to show mercy. That, women, has always been the true power held by emperors, kings, queens, sultans, tribal chiefs—even dictators and Supreme Leaders." She looked directly at Fidelity as she said this.

Fidelity replied, "That may all be well and good. That may all be well and good. But remember the wise saying, 'Women never forgive. Women never forget.' Discussion is over, honeys. I move for the public beating."

"Seconded," said Saridian.

6

Fidelity sauntered out into the arena where the gladiators were training. She brought her group of loyal women and subservient men—her most loyal men, her most trusted men. There were about eighty gladiators and their trainers present, so Fidelity ensured there would be no problems by seeing to it that there were an equal number of her best female guards, each fully equipped with modern weaponry.

Some of the women had guns, while others had tasers or lasers, and yet others had shockwave guns. Many wore exoskeleton load carriers, which allowed the female guards to carry heavy loads for long periods of time. Not only did the guards have modern weaponry, they had archaic ones as well: swords, knives, clubs, nunchakus. (The prevalent notion of the day, as written by the intelligentsia and promulgated by teachers from grade school to university, was that women had been denied weapons for so long that now it was their turn to wield such power. In any case, women were enamored with weapons.) To further ensure that things would go as planned—that is, that she could take Simon without incident—she also brought in about fifty men who would do much of the dirty work.

The gladiators were engaged in various forms of training. Some were working on strength, some were doing cardio, some were sparring. This was the perfect time for Fidelity to mete out her punishment to Simon Peter, because the real weapons were locked up during training. The men trained with heavy wooden swords, not real blades. The wooden swords were twice as heavy as metal ones, to give the men upper body and arm strength and to allow them to wield their real weapons quickly during actual battles. The weapons with which the men were practicing included swords, lances, tridents and nets, and bows and arrows.

Gladiator training was designed around fitness and acquiring skills with different types of weapons. Some gladiators were even training in how to die with the dignity befitting their class. There were specific rituals that must be strictly upheld. The women expected the men to die bravely and with honor, to show no fear. It was in this manner that the dying man would make his final tribute to the status quo and the leadership of women. By offering themselves up to cold-blooded murder, they were endorsing the matriarchy—the dominant position of women and the disposable position of men.

The gladiators were often spared death. More than you might imagine. They were too valuable; they had been too expensive to train. Slavery has always been an expensive endeavor. There were fights to the death, mind you. But those were largely left for less valuable men, or men who had offended the order of things. Men who had refused sexual service to a woman, for example. The rare moments in which a gladiator received a thumbs down was when Fidelity was present at the fights and when she was in an ill mood.

"Take him," Fidelity commanded.

A group of guards ordered the gladiators to put down their training weapons, while another division drew their swords and others aimed their rifles. It was a well-orchestrated arrest. They had practiced such maneuvers in the past.

Fidelity and her high-ranking guards approached Simon and ordered him to drop his training knife and to put his hands above his head. He complied without a struggle, but the look in his eyes spelled defiance. This did not go unnoticed by Fidelity, and it enraged her all the more. Sometimes a look can say much; your eyes can speak volumes without uttering a word. Two of the female guards took Simon's hands behind his back and handcuffed him.

"What's the charge?" glowered Simon. "I've broken no law."

"My dear," said Fidelity. "We don't rule by law; we rule by power."

The guards held Simon tightly and tied him to a pillar, while the other gladiators and their trainers could only watch sullenly.

John John was Simon's most loyal friend and it gnawed at his being that he could do nothing to help his friend. Not being free to act on your convictions was probably the worst thing about being a slave. He knew what was about to happen. He knew Fidelity's ways. He knew that when power was in the hands of a few, they ruled with impunity. But he could not risk trying to fight off the guards.

He was clearly outnumbered. He, like the other men, could only stand and watch. But he felt so demeaned, so emasculated. If he was not the biggest man in the arena, he was certainly one of the biggest and yet he felt like a eunuch.

Men were made to protect. Men were made to guard and to stand up for what they believed. If you took that away from a man, what was left? A shell. An empty shell. *That is what I am*, thought John John. *Just an empty shell of a man. I am not anything like Simon Peter. Never have been. Never will be. Simon inspires people; I just follow. Simon has charisma—well, I do have loyalty. There is something to that. Yes, that is what makes me a somebody, my loyalty to Simon. I feel like a hermit crab taking up residence in an empty shell. With Simon, I am something, and that is certainly better than nothing, which is what I am.*

Fidelity approached Simon, her cloak draped over her arm in a regal manner. "I don't owe you an explanation, but I will tell you why you are annoying to me. You are a trifle, like a mosquito. And I don't like mosquitos, they are a bother. And they can spread disease. I must not let the disease spread. I am a doctor, you see, and I will stamp out the disease. That is why we will make an example of you. And that is why I am telling you—because I don't want it to happen again. You will honor our culture, our society, our social order. You will not disrupt it by making your silly superstitious gestures," she said as she mockingly and incorrectly tried to make the sign of the cross. "You will make the sign of Matriarchy, you will honor the games, you will kill when I say kill, you shall yell 'Matriarchy Forever' for all to hear. In short, you will be obedient. Am I making myself clear?"

"Like ground glass."

"Do you think you can do that?"

"Well I am not in a position to argue with the queen."

The queen. I rather like that. "Do not refer to me as a queen," she said and slapped his face. "I am Supreme Leader, head of state. We are humanist, we are modern, we are progressive."

"Yes, our Supreme Leader, head of the state, head of the country, head of the world. I mean, we are a united world order, so...all the same thing. So yes, yes. I submit to you totally. You win. I lose. You are wrong and I am right. Oh, switch that...I mean I am right and you are wrong." He paused. He smirked. "Am I free to leave now?"

Fidelity laughed and walked away, making an ever-so-small gesture to her officers. A pair of women guards escorted her to her seat in the arena, while her generals ordered the men to "Teach Simon a lesson."

Two men were randomly selected to start the punishment. They were the useful idiots, the flying monkeys, the house slaves—take your pick. They were suffering from Stockholm syndrome; they believed in their own inferiority. Much like the knights of the medieval period and the teachers and professors of the 21st century, they fawned over the powers that be. Just as the knights loved their king and wanted his territory to expand, just as the educator loved his federal government and wanted governmental powers to grow and become more centralized, so, too, did the males in 131OW (the year 131 in the year of Our Woman) grovel at the sight, nay, the mere mention of women.

They had internalized the teachings; men were the weaker sex. Masculinity was toxic, was evil, so paradoxically, they began beating Simon about the face and gut. These men were not chivalrous, upright, respectable, productive, self-sacrificing men. How could they be? They had no role models. They belonged to a culture that did not respect maleness. They were empty shells of men, stunted in their growth by the conspiracy of the media, the schools and women at large. They lacked a moral compass; that was reserved for the noble women. They were not allowed to embrace masculinity, their abusers would not allow it, so they were emotionally stunted little boys who never grew out of emotional puberty.

They did the bidding of the ruling class women; winning women's approval was their only solace. Much like women of the 19th century and earlier were subservient to men, now it was so for men. Would humanity ever be ready to coexist respectfully? Not now, it seemed. Not now. Each man took his turn punching Simon in the face. The first tried his best, but it hurt his knuckles more than it hurt Simon. So the next man stepped up, but it seemed like Simon knew how to take a punch or had a granite chin, or both.

"C'mon, you feather-fisted sissy, show the women what you got," taunted Simon.

The two men glanced at each other. They wanted to show their mettle in front of the women, but they knew their fists were no match for his chin. So they switched it up and began to pound away at Simon's gut. Simon took a terrible beating, but he remained standing and defiant. As a matter of fact, it seemed like he had a little smirk on his face.

The men grew weary and slowed down noticeably, and their blows landed with less and less force. So the guards ordered them to stop. They looked up at Fidelity seated regally in her usual box seat, who nodded for two more men to complete the job.

The guards gave the men billy clubs to spare their fists and to get this over with quickly. These next two men stepped up eagerly. It's uncanny how witnessed behavior can change your own behavior. They began clubbing Simon, some blows landing on his head, some on his chest, his shoulders…one of the men even crouched low and thrashed at his thighs. When the guards ordered the ending of the beating, Simon stood tall and said mockingly, "You couldn't knock me down, fellas." Through blood and spit, he grinned widely and winked at John John and the other men who were observing the spectacle with discomfort.

The guards looked to their Supreme Leader once more, to see if yet two more men would be ordered to beat this guiltless man whose only fault was that he respected life and loved God so that he would not kill a man on the mere whim of the state. But Fidelity noted his defiance and was well aware that men were watching, so she ordered the beating to stop and for Simon to be untied. She had another plan in mind, one that would leave a lasting memory in the hearts and minds of the men (and women, for that matter) who even thought of a rebellious act. The job of the powerful, after all, is to keep power.

While Fidelity made her way back down from her seat to the arena, Simon stood with his chest puffed out and his head held high. He had never really thought of himself as a role model or any sort of leader, but now he felt he was being put into a position that was more important than himself. He was even bantering with the men who had beat him. At one point he said, "That was a proper beating, gentlemen. I think the women-folk appreciate what you did on their behalf and I think you saved yourselves from a beating. Well done."

It was at that point that the men realized that Simon Peter had been taunting them in order to spare their lives.

Fidelity walked briskly over to Simon Peter, who said, "The Supreme Leader enters. I would bow, but…well…under the circumstances…"

Fidelity did not let him finish. She shot him with an electroshock-wave gun, sending 100,000 volts of pulsing electricity throughout his body for a full ten seconds. Simon Peter stiffened and collapsed to the ground. When the shock was over, he had defecated on himself and the foul smell made the guards and men clear away. As he lay there in his stained clothing, Fidelity gave her weapon to a guard and ordered another guard to 3D-Snap him so that the state could post his image in the media, including all public monitors, and especially Sky Glass so that all could see what had become of the man who refused to make the sign of Matriarchy.

Fidelity and her entourage walked out of the arena. When they were in the hallway beneath the stadium seats, Colma stated, half matter-of-factly and half questioningly, "He looks badly beaten. Maybe he won't be able to fight very well."

"This may be preferable to him winning his next match. At least this way, we know we will have a fight to the death."

7

The next day, Simon Peter was prodded out of bed by the guards. He was badly bruised and battered, his nose was broken and he had a couple of cracked ribs. Regardless, the guards informed him that he would be fighting today. He did not protest. He did not say a word. As a matter of fact, he was not at all surprised. When the social order was as precarious as it was, and the power of the elite so tenuous, any slight to the powers that be was considered a potential catastrophic insurgency that must be squelched quickly and at all costs.

This was an irregular occurrence, however. Gladiators normally had plenty of time to train for an event and they knew they would be fighting for weeks, sometimes months, beforehand. There would be advertisements all over the public media and Sky Glass would display luminescent commercials in a full palette of colors across the sky, day and night, prior to a fight. Sometimes teasers would show both competitors' past fights. These teasers would be up to six or seven minutes long, and advertisements that long cost a lot of money. After all, to blanket the sky in a banquet of alluring brilliant colors, especially by day, pushed the boundary of mass media technological advances, and it attested to the world of commerce and the ascendance of the female class and its accomplishments.

Sky Glass was a seductive urban landmark whose signboard could be radiated anywhere, using the sky as a screen between two illumination towers which could be miles apart with the glittering show placed anywhere in between. There would be no radiant display for this last-minute battle, however. And the old rule of sparing the gladiators was thrown by the wayside. Fights to the death were normally left for the Undesirables, but Simon knew this was an exception to the rule and he accepted it with serenity.

Later that day, he was dressed in chain mail running down both his arms, a breast plate and armed with a longsword. As in his previous fight, he had no helmet. Also, he had no shield. He was the first to enter the arena. Standing there alone, looking up at the women, he felt daggers from the audience. How dare he disrespect women, he imagined them thinking. But he also noticed that a large minority seemed to be gazing upon him kindly.

Strange, he thought. *It must be my imagination. Not making the sign of Matriarchy is treason. And like Fidelity often says with pride, "Women never forget. Women never forgive." Leave it to Fidelity to turn a Christian teaching on its head. Fidelity does not have it in her to forgive even the smallest slight because she is weak. She may be the Supreme Leader, but deep down she is weak. Her power is the power of the state; her power is the power of the status quo; her power stems from the matriarchy. She has no power, no inner strength, to forgive.*

Simon Peter's thoughts were interrupted when his combatant entered the arena. The musicians played a majestic piece, Sky Glass splashed colorful images of him across the sky, and the women stood and cheered and threw him roses.

Simon Peter did not know him. He must have been sent in from a neighboring gymnasium. His name was Malcolm Andre. Simon knew this because Sky Glass rocketed his name in gleaming vivid colors. The sky-ad made it clear that Malcolm was undefeated, the best in his arena. *Women never forget. Women never forgive.*

This was going to be a simple sword fight. Normally, the fighters were purposely mismatched, one style fighting against another. Throughout human history, people had been curious to see which style was best, which country had the best techniques. Did kicks dominate fisticuffs? Was grappling better than elbows and knees? How did wrestling from Old Europe compare with Judo from Old Japan? How did a longsword compare with a sickle? How did a stun gun compare with mosquito drones? These were age-old questions that entertained women to this day.

But today would be an evenly matched sword fight; Malcolm Andre was suited similarly to Simon Peter. No matter, fights were not determined by style or by weaponry. Victory is mostly won by the fighter with the most heart, by the fighter who believes in his fight, by the best-trained fighter—with a bit of luck thrown in for good measure. Simon knew this from his years as a gladiator. He had seen that you could take two men, one clearly better than the other, and the better man would win, at most, seven out of ten fights. It followed, of course, that the lesser fighter would win three out of ten times. Nonetheless, Simon would put his confidence in training and conditioning. After all, those were things he could control. Serendipity was out of the realm of control.

After the fanfare, Malcolm and Simon met in the middle of the arena, swords at the ready. Each time the blades clashed, the crowd cheered and music bellowed. The men were evenly matched, but then Malcolm's dodge came a bit too late. Simon's blade met Malcolm's right ear and sheared it clean off. Instinctively, Malcolm dropped his sword and clutched at his ear—or where his ear should have been.

But instead of finishing him off, Simon, still holding his sword (he was no fool and knew that once you stepped into the arena, you must defend yourself at all times), picked up Malcolm's ear and demanded, "Ice. Ice. Put his ear in ice. It can be lasered back if we ice it."

This enraged Fidelity, who stood up and ordered her guards to shoot Malcolm dead. As the bullets flew, Simon flung himself to the ground to avoid being shot. But all the bullets were meant for Malcolm Andre.

The Supreme Leader then called out to have twelve more men enter the arena at once. This had never been done before. *I cannot let Simon Peter become a martyr, but if he dies in the arena as a gladiator, so be it*, Fidelity thought. She summoned the drone microphone, which hovered inches from her mouth, and said, "Only one man will survive. There will be only one victor, and there will be no agony in defeat because defeat will end in death."

Preeta quickly stood up and addressed her mother. "That is a brilliant idea, mother. Its function is twofold: one, it will squelch any uprising and show people the power of the state, and two, it will be highly entertaining. But mother, let me pick the men."

Preeta chose twelve men, one each with a short sword, a spear, a trident, a net, bolas, nunchakus, a sickle, a hammer, and shurikens. There was a boxer with brass knuckles, a man armed with a reflex bow, and another man atop a tall and majestic war horse who was also armed with a reflex bow.

Gladiator fights were the ultimate anachronism in 131OW. Before the Clone Wars, humanity had seen the invention of ships, bridges, automobiles, vaccines, antibiotics, to name a few. There were computers, cell phones, self-driving and flying cars; and after the Clone Wars, fusion reactors, artificially intelligent robots, sky screens, to name just a few. Modernity and science gave birth to many a great invention that improved lives greatly and yet the women yearned for days gone by, longing for masculine men.

Perhaps hundreds of thousands of years of evolution had produced a connection between men and women such that women sought the protection of men and men were eager to provide it. But men were so few, and subjugated so well for so long that few women even had an inkling as to their basic human instincts. Modernity has a way of masking nature.

Besides the entertainment value that the gladiator games provided, they also represented the dominance of women over men and there was value in that, too. You could say that Fidelity created an invention of her own that day, because never before had gladiators fought this way. The Supreme Leader spelled it out. "This will be a free-for-all fight to the death. Only one of you will be allowed out alive." She sat down. The rules of this new game were simple enough.

The men did not hesitate. The man with the bow and arrow who was not mounted retreated to the edge of the arena and sat down while the mounted archer used the flank of his horse to control some of the others.

Using the reins of his horse, the horseman rammed his horse's flank into the men, knocking down the ones equipped with the short sword, the trident, the shuriken and the net. It happened so fast. Simon Peter and the other competitors in this twisted game scurried out of the way.

The next two offenses happened almost simultaneously: the archer backed his horse away and shot at the man with the trident, while the trident fighter disentangled himself from the chaos of fallen men and thrust his weapon into the horse's neck. The archer's shot was true. First man down. The horse, trident in neck, was still standing, barely.

"My horse. My horse," he shouted to no one in particular as he shot his arrows into the shuriken, the net and the short sword fighters. Four men down. It all happened so astonishingly fast.

The other men looked around at the chaos and confusion. The eyes of the spear fighter and the brass knuckles and hammer combatants met and the man with the spear exclaimed, "We will fight soon. First the horseman."

The stallion collapsed to his knees, shrieking as it fell. But not before the archer let one more arrow fly into the man with the spear. Fifth man down.

"You will be organizing no attack on me," yelled the mounted archer. *How clever it is to team up with some of the others. That will increase my odds of survival.* This, however, was his last thought. Before he could speak, the hammer flew and knocked him off his saddle, and brass and hammer turned him into blood and mud. Sixth man down. The stallion scented blood and gave up on itself; it did not even try to get up. It just lay there.

The crowd cheered wildly.

Into the fray leapt the man with the nunchakus, attacking the brass-knuckled boxer. But another jumped into the melee, swinging his sickle in one long killing arc, putting all his tremendous power behind it, into the opponent swinging the nunchakus. Seventh man down. He trained his eyes on the boxer and did the same; the impact of sickle meeting neck sent a shock up his arm that caught him by surprise. Eighth man down.

Meanwhile, the bola fighter leapt into the carnage left by the stallion and his rider and untangled the net from the men. Now he had a bola and a net. *They have only one weapon. I have two.* Thus are the thoughts of desperate men.

Ironic, sometimes, the thoughts of men in battle. The mind can stray from thoughts of the past, lovers, fields of green, smells too. The comforting smell of foods, the pleasant smell of a roaring fireplace. The stride of a beautiful young woman. And, in centuries past, when the nuclear family was intact, and children were raised by mother and father, the number one reminiscence of warriors past was of mother. But all these were but a fleeting whisper of thought; a scintilla of pleasant distraction. The focus must remain in the here and now. At no other time is the mind more focused than in battle. Bola and net accosted sickle.

The crowd rose to their feet, frenzied in blood-lust. Fidelity remained seated, pleased with herself, knowing this was good for the women's morale.

The predator hurled his bola at his prey with an arcing, twisting motion of his right arm while holding the net in his left hand. The bola spun and wrapped itself around the legs of its quarry. Still standing, the sickle fighter tried to cut the bola rope, but the net found its mark and he was entangled in rope and net.

The hunter looked for a weapon, any weapon, and found the most conspicuous one among the carnage—the long spear. He took it and spun round quickly, spotting Simon seemingly for the first time. *The man with the sword or the man I have ensnared? Who first?* He chose Simon because the other man was incapable of harming him, at least for now, while Simon, who had been largely a bystander himself up to this point, had sword in hand. But the entrapped opponent screamed at his captor, "You will be next.

I swear upon the great Margaret Sanger, I will finish you."

Simon saw the spear sprout from the back of the ensnared man's neck. When he opened his mouth to scream again, only blood spurted out. He was dead before he met the ground. Ninth man down.

This all happened so fast.

Hammer and bola & net squared off, but looked askance at Simon. They nodded to each other as if to say, this one next. They came fast upon him. "Die," yelled the man with the hammer. "Die," they both began chanting in unison.

But, miraculously, an arrow pierced through the hammer man's throat. The word "die" turned into a croaking sound. Tenth man down. Only three left, including Simon. The screams from the women were deafening. The other man spun catlike to face the unmounted archer, the one who had seated himself on the ground. He was up now, walking toward Simon Peter and the other contestant. He shot the one who was not Simon Peter.

Only two men remained alive. The archer quickly approached the men who had been killed by the other archer, picked up the short sword, faced Simon Peter and…cut his own throat. Blood pumped, pumped, pumped from his neck, and spurted bright red on the ground.

The final tally was twelve men down. Simon Peter was untouched, like Daniel in the den of lions. He looked around at the fallen men—to his immeasurable disbelief, he was not one of them. He could not wrap his mind around the idea, the reality, that he was the last man standing. It seemed to him that they had been fighting from sunup to sundown, but in actuality, it had only been minutes. It had all happened so fast!

You can ask almost any warrior: in times of battle, time seems to stretch and shorten simultaneously. Movement seems at once to go...ever...so...slowly...and to skip from moment to moment like a strobe light at a dance party. And these two seemingly diametrically opposed realities are not a duality or contradictory at all; they both are true, they both happen at the same time. Time takes on a life of its own when death is but a moment away.

The screams from the crowd? Well, let's just say there had never been such an audience reaction in all the post-modern gladiator games. The music fell away. The band could not keep up with the pace of the action.

Fidelity stood up, spat contemptuously on the ground, and stormed away.

Yet the women cheered. Cheered at the spectacle. Cheered for a MAN.

Preeta stayed and cheered, too. She noticed, for the first time ever, that the male servants were as ecstatic as many, if not most, of the women and that the women were not stifling the men. Rather, it was a rare occasion indeed wherein the women and men were laughing, cheering, applauding and looking each other in the eye. Preeta even noticed some women hugging their male servants tightly and jumping up and down joyously in their arms. *Imagine that, laughing as equals*, she thought.

Later that evening, Preeta visited her mother in her private chambers over dinner. Fidelity had lost her appetite and she was clearly agitated. "That man has the audacity to think for himself. And worse, to act on his beliefs. This cannot be tolerated."

"What do you plan to do?" asked Preeta.

"We cannot turn this Simon Peter into a martyr. A martyr dies and his influence begins. We cannot allow that to happen." Fidelity played with her food thoughtfully.

"But what do you plan to do?"

Fidelity answered ruefully, "I must take matters into my own hands for the sake of the common folk."

"Which means what, exactly?"

"I will not involve the council. I will not make this a matter of the state. I will deal with this myself. I will have his food poisoned tomorrow morning. After he eats it, he will be fine for a few days, then he will get a fever and flu-like symptoms and die within a few days. It must be this way. We cannot make it known that he was assassinated or even died in the coliseum. It must be kept secret. It cannot leak. He is too dangerous as a martyr."

"Are you afraid of his ideas—what he stands for?"

"I fear no man. But we cannot have a slave rebellion on our hands. I am only thinking of our citizens; I am only trying to spare lives here. Simon Peter is too well-loved now. He is seen as some sort of hero. I cannot quite figure it out—I cannot even make sense of what happened in the arena! How did he survive such odds? And the man taking a knife... to himself!?! What is happening nowadays? I am perplexed, yet I know that once he has been eliminated, Pythia will be great again and we will have done our jobs as leaders and maintained the status quo. I cannot allow his death to be seen as coming from the hands of the state. His death cannot lead to martyrdom."

"It is not the death that makes the martyr, it is the cause. Do you fear that his cause is just?"

"Just? Just? Do you think it is justice to disobey the matriarchy? It is not a matter of course that a cause is right merely because a man dies for it. No. No. We must be done with him. We must be done with him. A woman never forgets. A woman never forgives. I have made up my mind."

"I see," replied Preeta. "I wish there could be some other way, but I see you have made up your mind and you only have the good of the state and our social order in mind. I wish you the best. May Sanger be with you. Good night."

PART
THREE

8

That night, Simon Peter was convalescing in his bed when Preeta, Savy and John John entered his room. Astonished at the sight of the three together, he could only sit up and stare. He knew something was amiss.

Preeta started, "Simon, I don't know how to tell you this or prepare you for this, so I will just say it. Time is of the essence here, so...I don't know how to begin." She looked to Savy for some assistance.

"I think you know me, I am the Secretary of State of Dworkin Province. We three met earlier this evening and Preeta informed us that your life is in danger. Fidelity intends to poison you in the morning. We want you to come with us. You are not safe here."

All four looked at each other for what seemed like an eternity. Simon had much to process and the other three were waiting for his response. He did not know what to say, though he knew it was his turn to speak. "John John, is this true?"

"I …I…don't really know. I trust Preeta, though. You should come with us right away. Let me get your stuff together," responded John John as he went to Simon's closet and began to put clothes into a duffel bag.

"What is going on here? You trust Preeta? What are you doing in their company?"

"I will answer that," said Preeta. "For years now, we have been planning an insurgency against Fidelity and her world order. We want independence and freedom for men and we will establish a new province in which men and women can live as equals and be judged by the content of their character. We hope to serve as a beacon of hope to the rest of the world, so that revolutions will occur across all of Pythia and true freedom and equality will spread throughout the planet. We have enlisted John John as a trusted man. He has been good to the cause, we think he is loyal. We trust him. As a matter of fact, we looked to him to be the leader of the rebellion. As you very well know, the men look up to him. He is well-liked, he possesses a disarming smile and, well, his physical stature." Preeta pointed to him and he stopped packing Simon's belongings for a moment, standing proudly to show his physique and to prove Preeta's statement correct. "But, and this is no slight to John John, actually he is the one who has been trying to tell us this—he lacks tactical decision-making and leadership skills. He has been trying to tell us that you have those skills, that you are that man. And now, after watching you lately, we agree. That is why you are important to us. We need you to come with us. We will lead you to safety."

Simon Peter let out a hearty laugh deep from his diaphragm. "That is not fair. I am in too much pain to laugh. This must be some kind of practical joke. Why you would stage such a prank, I do not know. But surely you must all be teasing."

"We are not playing with you. This is serious and we have no time to waste. You are to be poisoned in the morning. That is why you must come with us now," said Preeta.

"Oh, and where am I to go? Where is this safe place?"

"The No-Go Zone," chimed in Savy.

Still laughing, Simon snapped, "Now I know you are joking. The No-Go Zone is no place for life."

Savy replied, "That is the official position of the state. The truth, however, is the No-Go Zone is the rebel forces' central base. That area was ravaged with nuclear weaponry during the Clone Wars, and our state intelligentsia is under the impression that it is desolate, but our rebel forces live below ground.

The council conducts routine surveillance flights, but the thought of underground colonies has never crossed their minds. As far as they are concerned, the area is unlivable. There have been times that men have been spotted above ground hunting for food but these are rare occasions. They have been taught that if they are caught, they are merely to say they are runaways from nearby provinces. They are brought back to Dworkin, usually to the capitol here in Delilah, and summarily dealt with. Usually they are sacrificed in the coliseum, as you are well aware. But if the rebels and their families stay underground, they are safe. That is where you must go now. We can fill you in on the rest at a later date, after you are safe."

"We cannot even make our way to the No-Go Zone. The InterRegion is not conducive to human survival. It is overcome by global warming," Simon rebutted.

"Global warming," said Preeta, "was the biggest hoax ever perpetrated. In the mid-21st century, the governments of the advanced, developed nations lied to their people to procure taxes. It was the largest land grab in all of history. Surely, climate change is anthropomorphic—caused by womankind—but the solution, the people were told, was to tax them heavily. A carbon footprint tax, I believe it was called. Today, our government uses the same strategy to fool its citizens. And this global warming/climate change hoax served as a template for convincing women to unite against men—that men were evil and the reason for all of humanity's problems and that we need to be rid of the plague of men. I think they thought, 'If people will believe they ought to pay more and more taxes for something we know little about, then we ought to be able to convince them of anything.' It was powerful agitprop."

"No, climate change is based on science."

"Even at best, the science was flawed. It was based on computer models. Computer modeling should only be an adjunct to corroborating data in the real world. You can't predict far into the future with computer modeling. The data points are too chaotic to be known. Every variable could be close to infinity or zero, and that makes the expression meaningless. The scientific appearance is smoke and mirrors, but in reality, the system is chaotic and non-linear."

"But didn't scientists use means other than computer modeling?"

"For data collection, yes. But for the actual predicting...no. And even the data collection was spurious. The locations of temperature recording stations and the urbanization surrounding those stations over time caused temperature increases that they extrapolated to the entire planet. And even if warming was a trend, the alarmism was overwhelming. Warming trends need to be seen over the span of thousands of years. According to ice-core samples, the planet has been cooling and warming for epochs."

"But isn't Pythia experiencing radical climate change that people cannot accommodate? And isn't it caused by people?" Simon Peter asked.

"Yes," said Preeta. "But that is not the complete truth. For one, this may not be the case. Nobody can predict the future. Or, rather, we can only use math and science to create models that will help us see future trends—sort of like predicting the weather. But we purposely input faulty data to get faulty results, results that said what we wanted them to say. Also, these dire predictions failed to take into account that people could adapt to their environment. Humanity has done it for millennia. Mass migrations, using different materials, and using different sources of energy are just a few of the many ways that people adapt to a changing environment."

"But what if it changes too fast?"

"That is where the faulty data comes into play. That is where the governments tried—successfully, I might add—to scare the populace. It also happened in the late 19th century and early 20th century when it was feared that large cities like, say, New York City in what was once called the United States of America, would be overcome by horse dung. That having all those people living in high-rise buildings so close together would have too many horses concentrated in too confined an area. I think I remember that the mayor of New York paid for a so-called scientific study that showed that people would have to wade through three or four feet of horse dung on the streets and sidewalks. But you see, that did not happen because people invented automobiles. Automobiles replaced horses. No more horse dung. Voila, problem solved."

"And men played a big part in the invention of automobiles, don't you know?"

"It was mostly men, honey, it was mostly men. We in the liberation understand it was not men who were flawed, it was all of us. It is up to us as individuals to make the right decisions and choose between right and wrong. Simply put, you can have bad women and good men."

Simon's smile evaporated into pursed lips and a clenched jaw. Competing thoughts were flying randomly through his head, forming and reconfiguring like balls in a juggler's hands. He did not know which thought to focus on first. Only so many balls can be kept in the air at the same time. He chose a thought (if you could call it one thought) and voiced it.

"This is all too much to swallow. Revolutions? Freedom for men? Men seen as equals? Revolutions of freedom spreading all over planet Pythia? The No-Go Zone is a base for these freedom fighters? Why me? I have never been part of this."

Preeta answered, "You have shown leadership qualities for years now. For years, your allegiance to God, praying before a meal, and leading men in worship have inspired men who needed some hope in their lives. But lately, you have been something else. Your refusal to kill and refusal to cower to the

Supreme Leader have made you an instant legend. You have excited the women-folk like no one else in history. We think you are the one. You are the one who can lead us to freedom and equality."

"I'm trying to make sense of this. Women-folk don't like what I stand for. They don't like me upsetting the matriarchy. I pose a threat to their comfort and to the status quo."

"For some—for many, maybe—that may be true, but certainly not for all," Preeta explained. "Many of us are tired of the lies. We are tired of the manipulation. We are tired of the propaganda perpetuated by the government and by the media...but I repeat myself, the media is run by the government. We are tired of keeping quiet and not being able to voice our thoughts. We are also sickened by how we on Pythia reproduce asexually. And we can't even talk about it. Simon, listen to me, trust me, we are the hushed majority and we are tired of being voiceless."

"I see. But what makes you think that I can help? You women are certainly more educated than me, more well-spoken. I would probably lose to you in any debate. You need to find another."

"This is going to take more than mere debate. History has taught us that liberty comes at a price. We must fight so that the tyrants don't win," said Preeta.

"I think they already have."

"The final chapter has not been written. History is a morass, not inevitable. There have always been competing forces. There are competing forces today, but nothing is inevitable until after it happens."

"It sounds to me that you need some sort of hero figure. I am not that man. You must keep looking."

"No," retorted Preeta. "We have found the one, and he is you. We have decided. You are our answer. But listen, we have a time constraint here. This was not our original plan. We are a patient group. We had planned originally to observe you a bit more, and then to have John John plant seeds in your mind to prepare you for our vision and our revolt against the onerous system. We were going to groom you into our leader, but we must get you to safety now."

"I need to process…"

"I thought you said he was a man of action. I see no action here," Savy interjected.

"Ms. Noir," replied Preeta. "Did you not see this man of action in the ring? Did you not see how he carried himself? And how he dispatched all those men at once?"

"Well, he certainly had a little help in the ring, didn't he? He didn't fight the fight all alone," said Savy.

"What does that mean?" Simon asked.

"Tell him," said Savy.

Reluctantly, Preeta looked at Simon Peter and answered, "When Fidelity summoned the twelve men to fight in the arena at the same time, I did not know what to do. I was shocked; I had to think fast. I decided to pick the gladiators most loyal to our cause, with instructions to save you at all costs. As you can see Simon, they did. It came at a great cost; they made the ultimate sacrifice."

Simon reflected back on the fight, seeing it now from a completely different perspective. It was as if the first time he was fighting, he was fighting in the pitch black; but now that he was armed with this new information, the lights were on and he could see with clarity. The fighter with the bow and arrow who was mounted on the warhorse was certainly a freedom fighter. He did not notice it while it happened, but in retrospect Simon could see that the mounted fighter used the flank of the horse to protect him from the rest of the contenders. He recalled how the mounted gladiator finished the four men speedily and with seeming ease, even though Simon himself was exposed for the taking.

The image of the bowman shooting the spear man, even as the bowman was collapsing off his fallen horse, flashed in his mind's eye, bright like a Kodachrome picture. Clearly the spear man was not a freedom fighter. Nor, obviously, was the hammer man. The relentless beating of the formerly mounted man was a grotesque image that Simon quickly replaced with his newly-clear mental picture of the sickle contender yelling at the bola and net competitor, to distract him from assailing Simon himself.

Yes, upon review, the sickle combatant was on our side. And, of course, it was unquestionable that the archer on foot was a revolutionary, a brave soldier for a worthy cause. There was no other explanation for his behavior. The rebellion. That explained why he had taken his own life. Clearly he was a true believer, willing to die for the cause.

Simon felt silly for thinking that he had defeated the lot of them. He knew he was lucky, but he told himself that it took a lot of skill to be that lucky. Evidently, it was not providence; rather, it was Preeta's intervention.

Soberly, Simon Peter stood up and readied himself for the journey. Where he was going, he did not know. If he was prepared, he did not know. If he could succeed or be of some help, he did not know. He just knew that he did not want his fellow men, his fellow gladiators, to have died in vain. If they believed liberty for men was possible, it just might be so. If they believed that he could help them get there, it just might be so, and it was worth a valiant attempt.

Sometimes history picks men out and hoists them to higher levels even against their will. *God's plan shall be done with or without man's intervention; but in this case, man will help bring about God's will*, thought Simon.

9

After a bit more discussion and briefing, and waiting until the very early morning hours when most would be asleep, they started their escape to the No-Go Zone. They made it outside the gate without even seeing a guard. It was an easy escape. But Simon had a spontaneous idea, so he turned around and headed back into the coliseum.

"Where are you going? What are you doing?" asked Preeta.

"To get the rest of the gladiators and trainers," replied Simon as he increased his pace. Preeta chased him, overtook him and spun around right in his path, facing him. She hugged him tightly. "Please, don't do this to me, we must go."

"I must try to rescue the men."

Tears filled Preeta's eyes. "We need to get you out of here. Your life is in danger, not theirs."

"I owe it to these men; I have basically grown up with them. And besides, we can use them for your cause."

"Our cause," Preeta emphasized. "We have been keeping a careful watch on the other gladiators, too. We think they will fight for you, but not all of them have been vetted. We need to be more cautious and patient."

But Simon continued on. He went first to Alessandro Salvatore, the head trainer, who roused the other men and called them to order in no time flat. Still in the darkness of night, the entire gladiator school was outside the gate. Preeta had arranged for a Hummingbird car to pick them up. But there was only one; she had not anticipated so many gladiators.

"We need more Hummingbirds," said John John.

"I can hail them," replied Savi, looking intently at her comscreen. At this early hour, there were many cars available and because they were driverless, all you had to do was mapscreen one or hail it with your comscreen. Nobody actually owned cars; rather, they were owned by the state and used for rideshares. That is to say, they were subsidized through taxation of the population, regardless of how often you used them or if you used them at all. Only the Party members could own vehicles.

As the Hummingbirds silently arrived and self-parked in front of them, Preeta entered the one she had prearranged and commanded its computer to use buzz mode to fly east to the outskirts of the city. The flight would only take four or five minutes. From there, she thought, she could program the Hummingbird to enter the No-Go Zone. But the computer would not allow buzz mode. The Hummingbird screen read, "Sky Watch: airspace not available. Monitoring/Traffic Control not available."

"Humming won't allow buzz mode—says no airspace available," she informed the others, as she motioned with her hands to the sky to show that the skies were empty.

"At this hour of the night? How can that be? The skies are clear. Most everyone is asleep. There's no traffic at all," said Savi.

Alessandro interjected, "I will go get my horses. That will be good for twenty men."

Simon Peter admonished, "Don't be absurd. Horses in the street? That will surely draw attention."

"Look around you, Simon. Do you think we will go unnoticed as it is? The police will see us before we get to the outskirts. I would rather ride my horse anyway."

"I told you there were too many of us," Preeta moaned.

"Desperate times, desperate measures," Alessandro called back as he and some of his men ran back to get the horses.

The horses were ridden bareback; there was no time to saddle them up. Within twenty minutes, the caravan of grounded Hummingbirds and horses reached the perimeter of Delilah and headed one mile further into a deep valley, where they came to a dilapidated, long-abandoned town.

Relieved, Alessandro claimed, "See, my horses came in handy. We're there."

Simon Peter laughed and said, "Yes, I guess they did."

But Savi said, "Here is not there, and we're not there yet." Just then they were met with an onslaught of offensive tactical weapons. A bullet hit a wall behind them. And then another. And then another. Almost immediately, three and four more. Then a rapid bombardment. Shells were crashing all around them. The ground rumbled.

They were being attacked, but they could not see from where. Unceasing bombardment. They could do nothing but duck and lay low. The thunder of the guns swelled to a single indistinguishable heavy roar, an unbroken chain of sound, then faded into separate bursts of gunfire, then ceased...only to be followed by another barrage of heavy gunfire that again made one constant, long explosion.

During a quiet moment, Simon Peter yelled to the rest of the men and to Preeta and Savi to retreat behind a building. They did. Miraculously, nobody was hit.

"Fidelity must have known about the escape. Oh, how can I be so stupid. I'm sure your room must have been bugged," Savy exclaimed.

"That is how we got to this point so easily," cried Preeta.

"How many do you think there are?" asked Simon.

Savi replied, "Hard to say. From the sound of the artillery, I would say about twenty women or thereabouts."

"What are they armed with?"

"She didn't have time to organize a large militia. Not enough time to program the mosquito drones. They are probably just the city police force with handguns, rifles and machine guns."

"Are we gonna die?" cried one of the gladiators.

Simon turned around, ready to berate the man, but reconsidered when he saw that it was a young boy with tears in his eyes. He told the men to line up against the wall, shoulder to shoulder. He walked up and down the line and said with a gleam in his eye, "Look to your left. Look to your right. The one to the left and right of you will be injured, possibly killed, but I guarantee that you will come out unharmed." He winked and smiled at the men. It worked. They laughed.

They retreated up the empty valley, rode back to Delilah and were chased down by the city's police force. They created a barricade with the Hummingbirds and lay low behind the passenger cars. They faced east towards the empty town and the direction of their final destination, the No-Go Zone, with Fidelity's police force between them and their goal.

A shot rang out and a bullet hissed by Simon Peter's head. They ducked. He looked behind him.

"It came from a window in that building." Savi pointed.

"Smart. Never underestimate my mother," said Preeta.

Simon looked. *Fifth floor, front of the building, third window from the right.* "Give me your comscreen," he said to Preeta. "I will take out the sniper and whistle you when it is safe."

"No," said Preeta. "That building spells danger."

Savi said, "We chose him for a reason. He knows what he's capable of." Turning to Simon, she said, "Here, take this," reached underneath her garments and handed him a semi-automatic pistol.

"Ha, I don't know how to use those things."

"Here, I'll show you." Savi turned Simon around and, standing behind him, gripped the gun hand over hand. "You just point the gun at whatever you want to kill and squeeze this trigger right here," she said. "It will recoil, but I'm sure you can handle it."

"That's it?"

"That's it."

Simon took a helmet from one of the gladiators and carrying the gun, the comscreen and a short sword, made his way across the street to the building in which the sniper stood ready. There was a coffee dispensing kiosk on the sidewalk, and behind that was a patch of grass on the property of the rather large building. Past the lawn was a large circular driveway. It looked like an important building, like a hospital or an upscale hotel or the entrance to a successful conglomerate—or actually a combination of all three. It was huge, like a shopping mall. But it was unmarked. No signs. It seemed like a rather odd building to Simon, but, under the circumstances, he had other, more important things on his mind.

I will walk in through the front doors, take the stairs to the fifth floor, find the window, take out the marks-woman. He ran across the street and was met by two gunshots. He leapt behind the kiosk. *Where did those bullets come from? They can't be from the sniper, she's around the corner. More snipers? But where?*

He tested for the angle of trajectory and level of the shots with his helmet. He took it off and gingerly stuck it out on the edge of his short sword, dangling it just beyond the edge of the kiosk, facing the building. It was knocked from his hands by a bullet which ricocheted off another building across the street.

The helmet bobbled on the sidewalk in front of Simon. He picked it up, noted that the bullet had come in low near the rim, not high on the crown; and from that he deduced that the shooter must be low to the ground, not above. He looked through the glass doors of the entrance and saw shadows moving just inside the building. He took the gun from his pocket and aimed it at the figures. He fired four shots in rapid succession and the shadowy figures slumped to the floor.

No time to wait and see if they're dead. He ran up the walkway, opened the door, and entered to find two dead men. *I can see why the womenfolk don't let us have guns. They are not called the great equalizer for nothing.*

Simon walked down the hallway to a large in-door atrium. He looked up. He had to cock his head far back to view the glass ceiling high above. He looked right and saw a large, wide staircase made of marble.

He made his way to the fifth floor. He looked over the balcony down into the atrium. It was a hu-mongous enclosed courtyard, complete with trees, swimming pools, even a golf course. It was a wonder to behold. Simon Peter had never seen anything like it, not even in books. *In many ways, I have led a sheltered life.*

He entered what he thought was the correct room, an opulent suite that seemed as large as a house. He saw no one in the open area with the large kitchen, dining room and front room, so he opened a door thinking this might be the room with the window he sought. He moved down the hall-way and peeked into a few other rooms—an office, a library, a darkroom complete with photographic paper and chemicals.

That is truly an old art form. Goes back hundreds of years before the Clone Wars. Must be true art buffs.

He entered a bathroom and noticed something off. It looked like a normal bathroom with the usual toiletries, but there were men's and women's toiletries sitting side by side. Strange. He continued walking into the last remaining room. He was clearly in someone's master bedroom. He saw a man and a woman asleep together.

Strange. Men and women are not allowed to cohabitate.

He returned to the balcony. There he encountered a humanoid robot.

"What are you doing up at this hour of the night?" asked the robot.

"I attended a party," Simon replied. He paused to see if there was any reaction from the robot. There was none, so he was emboldened in his trickery. "It was a role-play party and I came as a gladiator."

"Oh, how fun," replied the robot. "Enjoy. Tell me if you need anything. I'm off to buy some spirits for my programmer."

That was a close one. It was only a domestic robot. A butler, really.

Simon Peter entered another door and inspected that domicile. It was the same configuration as the previous apartment, but when he reached the master bedroom, he saw the markswoman perched at the window, rifle at the ready, eyes peering through her scope, intent on her next kill. But not tonight.

Simon was a trained fighter. In the arena, he was stoic, calm, professional. It was his job to fight and if he must, to die with dignity. But tonight was different. He had never killed anyone. Could he?

Down on the street, he had not thought it through. What would he do once he found his shooter? Well, of course he must kill her. Right then and there, he made a choice; he flipped a switch in his brain and he allowed himself to rush back to primitive man, a thousand years earlier, when survival was paramount. He made a conscious choice to revert to his primal state, but once he did, he was not working consciously. He was in fight-or-flight mode, and that was far more reliable, more assured, less prone to error, and much quicker than conscious thinking.

Luckily for him, Simon Peter was now guided and protected by his newly awakened animal instinct, because the sniper sensed his presence. She turned around, rifle at the ready, but made the error of looking through her scope. It was not calibrated for close-range shots and it was too dark to see through it. Her use of the scope actually limited her vision; her training failed her in this instance. And in her profession, it only took one mistake to end a career and to end a life.

If Simon had not abandoned himself to his base impulse, he would not have become a part of history. But this was not his time to go to his final resting spot. Simon was a human animal, running on instinct. He lunged at the sharpshooter and buried his knife into her throat. That was all it took. *Stabbing your target repeatedly is for scumbag lowlife criminals.* It was such a simple action. And now this woman was dead.

It's a hell of a thing, killing someone. First they're here, then they're gone. I just took everything this person ever had, and ever will have. I am a thief, and I stole something of the utmost value that can never be returned. Not an easy thing, killing someone. So easy, yet so hard.

Simon realized he had people to protect, so he tried to shake it off. He took out the comscreen and called Savy Noir. Her 2D floating image appeared suspended in midair above the device. Simon did not want to be seen, so he turned off the visual.

"It's done. The sniper is...cannot hurt us anymore."

Just then he noticed a brigade of city police a few blocks west. "We are being ambushed. I repeat, we are being ambushed. There are eight to ten city police west of this building. We are stuck in between the police at the edge of town east of us and the police down the block west of us. Have John John lead twenty men north two blocks, then west four blocks, then back up to whatever this street here is. We will ambush the ambushers."

John John did as he was told, and they were successful. The police were not prepared for an attack from the rear. It was an easy matter for the skilled fighting men to overpower the police; even though the police were armed with firearms of all sorts, they were fixated on the men down the street to their east. The women were easily killed and their weapons taken.

Now the fleeing party had weapons of their own, including smart grenades. Thanks to myriad technologies like cameras, and heat-seeking and auditory sensors, these grenades were able to pinpoint and propel themselves toward their target up to fifteen feet away, such that you really did not need great aim or even have to time your throw before an explosion.

John John and his team rejoined the other party down the block. Simon met them there as well. Now that they were all reconvened, and more importantly unscathed, with high morale and confident that they could make their escape, they planned an attack. But apparently, Fidelity's forces had smart grenades, too. They came flying across their barricade of automobiles and wobbled on the ground before them.

There was no time to react. Within seconds, the grenades would launch themselves into the men, and into Preeta and Savi, indiscriminately, and detonate themselves. The larger bodies of the horses, however, attracted the heat-seeking monitors much more strongly than the humans could, and as it turned out, the grenades flew towards the horses and exploded.

The cries that ensued were not from humans; humans could not cry so terribly, so sickeningly. The cries of horses make the wailing of humans seem like whimpers. For the men and women trying to make their escape it was unbearable. It was the wailing of dumb, innocent animals—God's creation, who could not fathom the logistics of warfare or the inherent suffering therein. The horses were filled with anguish and terror, not able to comprehend their suffering. So completely, compellingly sad.

Alessandro Salvatore, who loved his horses the way a mother loves her newborn babies, screamed, "For Sanger's sake, shoot the horses. Please, please, for Great Sanger, take them out of their misery."

The threnody of the sentient animals grew louder. The hunted could not make out from where the bestial lamentations emanated; they seemed to be coming from all directions—north, south, east, west, above—everywhere. This was exacerbated by the fact that they were surrounded by high-rise buildings which acted like a man-made canyon of sorts that inevitably caught and reverberated all sounds, but more to the point, this was really a function of the cruelty that animals must suffer at the hands of humankind.

The feral weeping was omnipresent and seemingly never-ending. It persisted unceasingly. The harrowing cries of the totally innocent animals permeated and saturated into the eardrums of the humans, everywhere. The cries seemed to emanate from every direction, but they were not from men, they were not from women, they were only from horses, which made it all the more inhumane.

Alessandro could bear it no more. He screamed in a high-pitched voice full of anguish, "They are Pythialings, like you and me. They feel like you and me. Take them out of their misery. Oh, I should not have brought them with us. I should not have introduced them to the affairs of the human race. Take them out of their misery. Take them…"

A shot rang out from the east, from among the policewomen. Alessandro was dead before he hit the ground. In his heartbroken state, he had exposed himself above the Hummingbirds and made himself an easy target. One careless mistake is all it ever takes.

Savi took a rifle from one of the men and crouched on one knee, pointed her weapon at a horse that was only wounded and fired. Mercifully, the horse dropped. Savi aimed at another, whose belly was ripped open with his innards spilled on the ground, and shot. Savi pointed her rifle at another. This horse slipped and fell on its own innards, but stood up again, mouth open, emanating tormented calls for help. Another shot. Savi aimed at another horse whose hips and spine seemed to be broken and was crawling around on its forelegs, dragging itself across the street. She fired, and it was freed from its suffering. It was in this manner that

Savi stifled the cries. All was quiet save for the recent memory of the screams of the completely crimeless creatures.

10

Things were looking dire for the fleeing group. Simon Peter had to think of something quickly. Still laying low, he went over to Alessandro, bent down over the body and made the sign of the cross and said, "Yes, your horses came in handy, my friend. And thank you for giving us your children. I will see to it that they did not die in vain."

He made his way back to Preeta, Savi and John John. He said, "I have a plan. We take half our men and fall back west down this street. A fourth of us go north; a fourth of us go south down this street here. We wait it out. When the police come in, they will find Alessandro. We will send him a note. They will think that we think he is still alive. The note will say something to the effect that we went around their guard and will attack from behind them, from the east. They will continue west. At that point, we will block them at the west end, and the north and south contingents can circle back and get them from the east. They will be surrounded."

They did exactly that. They left the barricade of autos, the horses and Allessandro's body there at the intersection, and went on foot to their new strategic locations. Even though Simon Peter told Preeta and Savi that they would be safer if they went with the north or south team, the women chose to go west towards town with him.

And there they waited. It was still dark, and they appreciated that. A surprise attack following their apparent retreat would be more efficacious under the cloak of night than under the exposition of light.

While waiting, Simon mentioned his experience in the large, strange building in which his sniper hid. He purposely avoided talking about the woman, and especially that he had killed her. Rather, he concentrated on the immensity of the structure, and the beauty of the inner chamber, but mostly he talked about seeing a man and a woman living together, seemingly sharing a house. "Isn't that strictly forbidden? And doesn't the government have ways to thwart such a forbidden activity?"

Preeta put her hand on his shoulder and said, "After we arrive safely in the No-Go Zone, we will have many things to teach you, but for now, to answer your question: Yes, the government has a plethora of ways, both low-tech and high-tech, to catch such criminals. But there is an exception; an exception only for the rich, of course. Just like all throughout history, we have one set of laws for the common people and one set of laws for the elite. There was a short period of time during the 19th and 20th century, before the Clone Wars—in only some countries, mind you—that tried to make things more egalitarian. And they were largely success-ful. Probably the best example of that was in the United States of America, which is the very land where we stand now. It was a beacon of hope for the rest of the planet. But during the 21st century, those advanced countries started falling apart, be-gan devolving hundreds, even thousands of years in their thinking. Those countries could not withstand the internal protests of its own citizens; they failed from within, not so much from any outside enemies. Well, that is hard to say. Those countries let in too many unvetted foreigners who had no intention of assimilating and they were coming in too quickly to acculturate. Don't get me wrong, we welcome people from all cultures, religions, ethnic backgrounds, etc. We feel, however, that the people coming in need to commit to our values and way of life, not try to sub-vert us. And anyway, the schools were teaching them to hate their newly adopted country altogether. It was a recipe for disaster. As I often say, 'If you bring them here, here becomes there.' And to make a long story short, things have gotten much worse now."

"I don't understand," said Simon.

Preeta got to the point. "Rich women go to the 'Love Factory,' as most of the upper-class women affectionately refer to it. The government refers to it as Area 54, for some reason I do not know. There they have more traditional relationships with men, and the women actually get pregnant and have babies the natural way. This is a means to create the strongest and healthiest offspring, but only for the elite."

"Do the women live with the men round the clock?"

"No, they go in and out as they please."

"But then how can they hide their pregnancies for nine months?"

"They don't need to hide their pregnancies for the full nine months. A woman naturally does not show for the first couple of months but yes, you are right that they do have to be gone for some time. That is all part of what the women pay for. A vacation or sometimes even a supposed job relocation is used to hide the pregnancy."

"I see, so the men are used as stud bulls. I will go back there and free the men and they can also fight for us."

"That would be an exercise in frivolity. We freedom fighters have looked into this for years now. They would most certainly not join our cause. They enjoy too many privileges. They are treated as equals. They get to raise their children in luxury. They have the freedom to travel. They are rewarded handsomely for their services. And, mind you, they are not being paid for sex; rather, they are being paid to not talk about it."

"I see, they are house slaves—they love their mistresses."

"Yes."

At that moment, a drone flare flew high above the intersection east of them where the barricade stood. A blue-green light bathed the area. It lit up everything around the intersection, and Preeta, Savi and the rest of them saw shadows sharply outlined in the street.

"Damn, how long is that going to be up there? We cannot make the smallest movement without being seen."

Preeta replied, "Such a beautiful glow, if it wasn't so dangerous. Is the sky becoming lighter on the horizon, or is it my imagination?"

"Trump, we don't have much time," Simon grunted.

11

Fidelity and her team cautiously reached the barricaded intersection. With flashlights and guns drawn, they inspected the area. They saw the dead horses and Alessandro fallen nearby.

Fidelity laughed at her success. "Well, comrades, it looks like they are running away. I want the men dead or alive. The women, alive. There will surely be a raise for the lot of you, and vacation time added on, too. Remember, women, guns don't kill people, people do. But the guns help!"

She laughed again. Just then, Simon sent a message to Alessandro's comscreen. One of the police read it aloud. "Ride horses as diversion, while we circle round east to attack from the rear."

The women panicked. "They are planning an attack from the east," said one officer.

"They don't know the horses are dead," screamed another.

"We must retreat west down Central Street," said a third.

Fidelity suspected that all was not right. After all, she was not Supreme Leader for nothing. Her lighthearted, haughty demeanor changed and she commanded her troops in a cold voice. "Women, we will retreat west into town down Central Street. He who fights and runs away lives to fight another day. Matriarchy forever."

The police squad gladly abided by Fidelity's wishes. She, however, remotely shut off the drone flare. *If I make it easier for the men to capture my police, I increase my likelihood of escape.*

She traveled east out of town and got into her own personal Hummingbird and put it into buzz mode. The exhaust blasted against the ground, and the VTOL, or vertical take-off and landing, Hummingbird car went skyward, then the thrust switched from below the car to behind it and it took flight straight away, like a hummingbird. Fidelity escaped. But the same could not be said for her police force.

As they marched west down Central Street, arms at the ready, surveying left, right, and upward, watching for surprise attacks, Simon ordered his team to circle back from the north and south. The police were trapped. They had nowhere to run. They were clearly surrounded and outnumbered. While the policewomen were looking askance and confused, not knowing what to do next, Savi called out, "You have no more Supreme Leader, she has abandoned you. Put down your weapons now and we will not harm you."

"How can we believe you?" an officer called out.

"We are not here to kill anyone. We are only trying to get these men to safety," answered Savi.

"We know you have killed at least one already," the same officer countered.

"That was unavoidable," yelled out Simon. "She was trying to shoot us. Lay down your weapons now, and we will take you with us. We will not mistreat you in any way. You have my word on it. If you do not cooperate, we will shoot to kill. You have five seconds to decide. Five…four…three…"

The policewomen laid down their weapons and the skirmish was over before it even started. The best outcome of any conflagration is surrender with no casualties. Any military officer will tell you that. Fighting is the last resort of any true fighting man or woman.

Day began to break over the horizon; a soft golden glow appeared just over the hills to the east, the direction of their escape. It was still dark where they were; the light hadn't yet reached them. Simon looked at the spectacle and said, "Funny how escape is toward the light. I think God is lighting the way for us."

"Escape is always towards the light of truth," Preeta added. "Let's get to the VTOLs."

"First let me take a few men and see if there are any additional women hiding back at the barricade. At this point, I do not want to take anything for granted," said Simon.

"Good idea," said Preeta. "Savi and I will join you."

Simon's team performed their reconnaissance, found everything clear and marched back to the group and the captive police officers. The sun had risen completely over the hills by now; the city was fully illuminated. The day had finally broken.

When the scouting team arrived back to the group, they saw that the men had formed a large circle in the intersection. They were crowing and cheering. Simon heard one of the men say to another man, "Should we give them the thumbs up or the thumbs down?" They laughed. Simon was not sure what that meant, but he had a hunch.

When he broke through the crowd, his suspicions had been confirmed. He was heartbroken to see that, only minutes into their newfound freedom, the men had armed two women with short swords and forced them to fight.

Simon placed himself in the center of this crude ring. That was all that was necessary. The roar of the men died down, and they all stood waiting for him to speak. With a sorrowful expression, he took the weapons from the fighters and called out to the crowd, "We must be better than this. If we treat the women the way they treated us, inequities and atrocities will never end. We will only be substituting one oppressor for another. There can be no justice without forgiveness. If we drink from the cup of bitterness and hatred, we will only be spreading bitterness and hatred, we will be unable to create an egalitarian society, and we will perpetually thirst for freedom and equality. Men and women alike must realize that we are inextricably linked. We men must serve as role models, practice self-control, respect for women, and restrain ourselves from physical violence and the degradation of women. We must be on the right side of history. We must be better than that. We are not savages, after all."

The men were ashamed of their behavior and promptly, yet dejectedly, dispersed. They made it back to the VTOLs and, because they were outside of the city perimeter, they were able to engage buzz mode.

During their flight to the No-Go Zone, Preeta congratulated Simon on his speech. "You have made me proud. I think you have solidified yourself as leader of the emancipation movement."

"Thank you," Simon responded. "I would not go that far, but thank you. I just think it comes from my belief that there are three main types of calamities in this world. The first are natural disasters, like floods, typhoons, hurricanes, Pythiaquakes and such. The second are diseases. And the third are man-made problems, like slavery, war, communism. I feel strongly that the last set of problems, the human-made problems, can be overcome. We created those problems; we can ameliorate them and even eliminate them." He paused, then continued. "So it really bothers me when I see people harming other people in any way. It is, simply put, just not right."

The VTOLs landed in the No-Go Zone. They had made it. They were safe. For now.

PART
FOUR

12

As the Hummingbirds landed in a tight formation within the boundaries of the No-Go Zone, Simon Peter looked out across the desolate landscape. Flat, arid, not much sign of plant or animal life.

They landed on a very flat piece of ground. Even though there was nothing of note in the landscape, Simon let out an audible grunt. After all, it was not every day that you saw the ground below you gently give way. But that was precisely what happened. The large rectangular piece of ground on which the Hummingbirds rested descended underground like an elevator platform.

Simon's uneasiness was assuaged by Preeta gently patting his knee and smiling knowingly at him. He correctly read her demeanor as saying, yes, we are in control; this is part of the plan.

When the platform reached the bottom of its travel at the floor of the cavern, the cars drove off and the platform ascended into its original position.

The fleeing party exited their vehicles and Simon Peter said to Preeta, "It's so vast."

Preeta laughed. "Yes, it took years to build. With money and materials I have secretly siphoned from the Unified Governments, we used massive tunnel boring augers and other mining machines to create what is essentially an underground city—we call it New America. We have electricity generated by fusion reactors, so we have lights that can essentially duplicate sunlight. We use that manufactured sunlight to mimic the outdoors. We programmed the lights to create night and day to match our circadian rhythm. We can grow fruits and vegetables in our underground gardens. We can even go for walks or play in our park—we call it Central Park—and get our daily dose of vitamin D. Most importantly, it cannot be detected by the World Government. This is where we live naturally, men and women living and working side by side. And this is where we launch our fight for independence and begin to set the rest of the world free. This is where we make ready and prepare you to become the leader of the resistance."

"It is so vast," Simon repeated. "It's so vast." A man can only take in so much at one time.

"Yes," Savi answered. "It makes subway tunnels and highway tunnels seem like gopher holes by comparison."

Preeta escorted Simon Peter to the New America Hospital, where the staff tended to his wounds, suffered from the mistreatment he'd endured at Fidelity's hands. During his convalescence, Simon spent most of his time with Preeta. She was his field guide, so to speak, helping him to discover New America and introducing him to new ideas not taught by any school on Pythia.

For weeks, Preeta checked in on Simon daily. They went on long walks together, often through the city park. She prepared all his meals, and they ate together. Even though she had many responsibilities in New America, both as its democratically elected president and as a key organizer of the liberation, she always found time for Simon.

She put him up in one of the best residences in New America, right next to the White House, which was really a wood and stucco dwelling in the center of the cavern, where Preeta herself resided when she was in New America. She showed him the layout of the city, with its many dwellings etched into the perimeter of the cave, many of which were two- and even three-story homes where the constitution of the cave allowed for building vertically into the structure without disrupting the integrity of the walls.

She gave him a tour of the government buildings and the downtown area, complete with shops and small parks. These were built in the cavernous center of New America. She showed him where they grew food. She showed him their natural underground river. The original engineers who built New America considered it a stroke of luck that the place they had chosen to build below ground had a natural underground river flowing through it. They just had to make sure that they did not disturb its natural flow. They called the river the Mississippi.

Preeta took him out to downtown restaurants, and accompanied him to classrooms at the city school to witness children, girls and boys too, learning and growing together. It was during these few weeks that Simon Peter began to entertain the idea that he was, in fact, smitten with Preeta. After all, she was treating him like a complete person. *She is proving herself to me*, he thought. She was actually listening to what he had to say. They had many interesting conversations. She was taking him seriously. Never before had any woman taken such an interest in him, other than for his body or his fighting skills.

A few weeks after their arrival in New America, Preeta showed him the garden where they grew vegetables and fruits. He asked her why they didn't eat meat of any kind in New America—no beef, no chicken, no turkey, not even fish. "The animals are sentient Pythialings like you and me. We are sharing the planet with them," was her answer.

"But don't you need the protein?" asked Simon.

"We can get the protein we need without eating flesh. If they have parents, we don't eat them. If they have eyes, we don't eat them."

"But isn't being a vegan difficult?"

"Not nearly as difficult as being a farm-raised animal who is about to be slaughtered."

"That's funny."

"Thanks. I just don't want my body to be a coffin for other living beings."

"Ouch, that's not so funny."

They continued walking through the garden, variously eating strawberries, green peas, pulling up carrots from the ground and eating them unwashed while chatting. They talked about many things, yet kept their topics rather innocuous. At one point, Simon asked her to stretch her hand out, extending his own arm straight out with the palm down to demonstrate. She complied and he reached out and took her hand in his and said, "Perfect fit." She smiled and they continued their stroll.

13

few weeks after that, Preeta invited him to visit some classrooms to see how and what their children—ranging from five to seventeen years of age—learned. When they entered the eleven-year class (so-called because that was the modal age of the children), the pupils were studying music appreciation. They would listen to a great classical composer from the past and then would guess the composer's name on their Sky Tabs. When all the students had made their guess, Sky Tab would display the answers in mid-air in front of the class, in a fashion quite similar to Sky Glass; after all, both the technologies were developed by the same company.

After the guessing phase, they would discuss some key elements of the piece, then learn a bit about the personal life of the composer before moving on to the next composer. This was a great way to make music relevant to the students.

The first piece was Ludwig van Beethoven's Fifth Symphony in C Minor. The children were listening intently, many with intense looks on their faces that matched the fierce music. When the voting had been tallied, Preeta laughed that there were many in the class who did not know the composer. Simon, however, did not laugh. He had never heard this piece of art. Art made by men, especially by old White men, was actively suppressed by the government.

They discussed the "short-short-short-long" opening of the entire exposition. The teacher asked the class to compare that motif in the first movement with the same motif in the fourth and final movement. The astute listeners declared that the four notes at the beginning of the piece were "sad," while the same motif was "kind of happy" at the end. That brought up a discussion of minor versus major keys.

The teacher explained to them that during the time that Beethoven wrote the piece, it was incumbent upon the composer to close the arrangement in the same key as the opening passage; yet Beethoven chose to change keys. It was in this manner, and because he chose to express his emotions boldly with pieces that moved in surprising directions, and not follow the customs of his day to present pieces that were symmetrical and balanced, that Beethoven ended what was known as the Classical Period and gave birth to the Romantic Period. The teacher also intrigued the students with facts about the composer himself, that he wrote most of his compelling work while completely deaf and that he contemplated suicide, but chose life over death due to his love and respect for art.

"I would have ended my life—it was only my art that held me back. Ah, it seemed impossible to leave the world until I had brought forth all that I felt was within me," the teacher read from a letter written by the composer himself.

Simon leaned over to Preeta and said, "Not only is he teaching music appreciation, he is subtly teaching that men are to be respected and that men have contributed a lot to humanity." She smiled.

The teacher played pieces by Mozart and by Chopin. Again, they discussed the structure of the music and the personal lives of the artists. The students were surprised to learn that both Mozart and Chopin had died young—thirty-five and thirty-nine, respectively. One girl called out, "How could they have possibly created so many works of beauty at such a young age?"

Simon, too, was inspired when he heard the teacher say that Chopin stopped playing mid-concert when a Russian occupier of his native homeland, Poland, entered the parlor. "I do not play for Czarist butchers," he was purported to have said. Refusing a Russian passport, Chopin was forced to flee his homeland, never to return. He paid a price for his allegiance to his people, and Russian troops even destroyed the piano he had played in Warsaw, throwing it out a second-floor window as some sort of symbolic revenge for the failed Polish uprising.

The students were treated to Florence Beatrice Price's Symphony in E Minor, which, they were taught, was the first symphony by a Black American woman to be played by a major orchestra. And this was in the early 20th century, a period of great racial division in America, and a trying time for African-Americans due to laws and social norms. At the time the music was written, there were laws forbidding Black people to vote, there were separate schools and facilities for the descendants of Black Africans, and there were lynchings. At this school in New America, the mistreatment of Black Americans was often compared to the mistreatment of men after the Clone Wars.

Preeta was due to meet with other leaders of the rebellion and she wanted Simon to see a class of older students, so Preeta and Simon decided to leave the class. As they were leaving, the teacher played a composition called "Maggot Brain" by George Clinton, another Black American composer of the late 20th/early 21st century, to introduce the students to a unique and clever interpretation of a piece of art written in the form of a waltz.

Upon leaving the classroom, Preeta said to Simon, "The Fifth symphony of Ludwig van's is bold and strong and expresses Beethoven's extroverted side."

Simon Peter asked what the word "extroverted" meant (there were holes in his education).

Preeta wisecracked, "It is like you."

Simon thought on it for a moment, and then said, "That doesn't tell me much."

Finally, Preeta answered, "That it's out there for all the world to see."

14

A few weeks after that, Preeta received an alert that someone had ventured above ground out of New America without prior approval. This was dangerous—for the individual and for all the residents of New America. What if there was a state-run patrol or fly-over? Heaven forbid that someone was found out who could lead the powers-that-be to New America. People were allowed to go above ground, but that was seldom done. New America's Defense Team would survey the landscape and appraise the situation, making certain that it was safe for the inhabitants to leave their underground safety. And what is more, they were always prepped before they were allowed to venture about. For example, if they were ever caught, they were instructed to say that they were from nearby provinces. Before approval was given, there had to be good reason to risk being found out. Good reasons included foraging for food, or, in Preeta's case, to be allowed to go back to Delilah to keep up pretenses with Fidelity.

But in this case, none of that had occurred.

Preeta was going to let her Defense Team bring the New America citizen safely back home, but when she learned that it was Nova Seralda and that the young woman was with child, she decided to take matters into her own hands. She took a few of her best Defense Team soldiers with her and went to Nova's home. They found her husband, Hector Ernest, poring over Nova's handwritten notes. When the team entered, he knew the reason for their intrusion. Leaving New America without permission put everyone in danger, he realized. With no perfunctory nods or greetings, he read aloud from her notes, "A quote from Margaret Sanger, the founder of the Planned Parenthood Federation of America, whom we named our country after, the United Governments of Sanger: 'The mass of Negroes particularly in the South still breed carelessly and disastrously, with the result that the increase among Negroes, even more than among whites, is from the portion of the population least intelligent and fit, and least able to rear children properly.' And 'We do not want word to go out that we want to exterminate the Negro population and the minister is the man who can straighten out that idea if it ever occurs to any of their more rebellious members.' Don't kid yourselves, the main goal of the abortion movement was always so-called 'Negro eugenics,' the control of the Black population in what was once called the United States of America. In her autobiography, Sanger proudly recounted her address to the women of the Ku Klux Klan in Silver Lake, New Jersey, in 1926 AD before the Clone Wars. But nonetheless, I want autonomy over my body."

"What are you reading?" asked Trulia, sergeant of the Defense Team.

"I'm reading her notes. They are about the pro-life/pro-choice debate. She has two columns, pros and cons. She left New America to go back to Delilah to get an abortion."

"OK, I have heard enough; I understand the situation. We must leave now. Hector, you come with us," Preeta ordered.

It did not take long to catch up to Nova. She had not gotten very far.

Hector called to her. She wept and said, "I'm sorry I brought you all above ground. I just cannot go through with this."

"But we've talked this over. You have told me that we as a culture respect life and that we respect life so much that we do not even eat animals. Can't you see the contradiction between not killing animals, yet killing nascent human beings?"

"Of course I've considered that. I've been pondering over this all of my waking hours, asking myself what the right thing to do is."

"And you've concluded that killing the baby inside of you is the right thing to do?" Preeta asked.

"With all due respect, Preeta, lighten up here," Hector rebuked.

"She's a grown woman," said Preeta. "She can handle it."

Hector turned to Nova. "But why?"

"I am afraid. I'm scared of what might happen to my body. I'm scared of dying."

Preeta answered, "What makes you think you will die?"

"I've read on our history sites that many women have died during labor."

"There still exists a slight risk, but you are citing statistics from hundreds of years ago. I promise you, Nova, we will have the best medical care that New America and modern medicine can provide."

"How can you say that? We have had so few natural births. I have heard of natural births still existing, but it is all just a rumor. I don't know any woman who conceived the old way."

"I can introduce you to some women who have given birth the old way. They exist."

"I don't think that endangering the life of the mother—of me—is of any concern to you. I need to go to Delilah and get a legal, compassionate abortion."

"'Compassionate', you say. You are not being compassionate to the baby."

"It is not a baby. It is not a real person."

"What is it, then? A tree? A frog? Science and philosophy and religion all agree that that person is indeed a person. You are either a person or you are not. And if you are a person, you have a right to life. Period. It is binary. You are either a person or not. There is no spectrum. Just like the distinction of gender and sex is binary—you are either a man or a woman. There is no spectrum when it comes to personhood, and there is no spectrum when it comes to a man or a woman. If gender is not binary, then show me one human being in all of human history that has the reproductive ability of both sexes. Show me one person that can get itself pregnant. Color is a spectrum. If you mix red with yellow you get orange. And if you mix red with yellow in different proportions, you get different shades of orange. Where are the different shades of orange in human sexuality? There is none. We only have red and yellow. Period. Men and women. So orange can be on a spectrum, but not gender or sex and not personhood. Period."

"Why do we call a baby in the womb a fetus, then? Why do we have that word?"

"Because it is a useful word. It names the distinction between an unborn human and a born human, but that distinction is irrelevant when you are discussing killing it. We live not only in space—you are there and I am here—but also in time. We live in time such that that person will be a fetus, then a toddler, then a child, then a teenager, then an adult, then an elderly person. But if you kill it, that ends the natural progression of maturity over time. The only distinction that matters is: Is that person a human being? That it is an embryo, or a fetus, or a baby is all irrelevant. Is it a human life? That is the only question that is relevant here. And if it is not a human being, then why did Planned Parenthood harvest organs from it? We are always an incipient or progressing or growing life—unless you kill us, of course. You don't have a right to quote-unquote 'end a pregnancy,' but you do have a right to prevent a pregnancy by not getting pregnant in the first place. If you don't want to produce a baby that you are going to kill in the womb, then don't have sex with that person. You, Nova, are beyond that point."

"But babies are not independent," Nova shot back.

"Well what about a six-month-old baby? They are not independent, either. What about somebody in an iron lung? Should we kill them, too?"

"But babies aren't self-aware."

"So now you are talking about sentience. What about people in a coma? They are not sentient. What about somebody who is sleeping? Should we kill them, too? Maybe we should just be able to kill someone if they disrupt our standard of living."

"No, I am not saying that, but should a woman be forced to reproduce?"

"Of course not, but should a woman be allowed to kill what has already been produced?"

"If you are in a burning building," Nova replied, "do you save the mother or do you save the child?"

"That is not a good analogy. A better analogy would be: If you are in a burning building, would you kill the baby?" After a long pause, Preeta concluded, "You see, there really are no good arguments for killing an innocent unborn child."

"I appreciate what you are trying to do here, Preeta, but I am not stupid. I have been considering this for a long time now. I am aware of both sides of the issue. And there is an excellent argument for being pro-abortion. And that argument is that I get to have autonomy over my own body. My body, my choice. Government does not have a right to control me, to choose for me. I get to make my own decisions as a respected member of society. No argument is better than that."

"Yes, you are right. Your body, your choice. But this situation is more complicated than that. There is a countervailing interest here; the life of the baby. Just like you can tell the story of the Wizard of Oz from Dorothy's point of view or from the point of view of the Wicked Witch of the West, you can tell the story of abortion from the mother's point of view, in which case it is a happy ending for the mother—and often the father, too—or you can tell it from the point of view of the baby, in which case the ending is tragic."

"And if I go through with this, the ending could be tragic for me, too. You don't seem to care about endangering the life of the mother. That concept is foreign to you."

"Like I told you, having this baby will not endanger your life, but you know what endangers the life of the baby—abortion. The question basically comes down to, 'Is human life worth protecting?' If it is not, then you need to present a good argument as to why some life is worth protecting while other lives are not. It is really a moral question and one that determines the course of a culture. You cannot kill the innocent unborn and have a moral basis to make any other arguments."

"OK then, no more arguments from me," Nova said as she turned and walked away from the group toward Delilah. "I have made my decision."

Hector caught up to her and said, "Just hear me out. Come back home with me. I want to show you something meaningful to me. If, after that, you still want to get...you still want to go to Delilah, I will petition the Defense Ministry myself on your behalf, and I will personally escort you to Delilah."

She assented. The entire group made their way back to New America without incident, and when Nova and Hector reached their home, he escorted her to the basement while they continued their discussion regarding abortion and the right to life.

He turned to her and said, "Abortion is like slavery and the Holocaust."

"And why do you say that?" Nova scoffed.

"Because the slave owners said that Black people were not people, they were private property. Slave owners took away Black people's humanity, took away their personhood. And the Nazis said the Jews were not people. To the Nazis, Jews were subhuman. Before you can abuse a group of people, you have to dehumanize them. That is what abortionists do with babies, they say babies in the womb are subhuman."

Hector sensed that she remained unconvinced, but that she was more open to this line of reasoning than she had been above ground. So he continued, "If it is wrong to own humans, it is also wrong to kill them. Oh, but they are not people, the abortionists would say. But who has the right to say such things? To racists and anti-Semites, Black people and Jews weren't people either."

Nova shifted her feet. "If you are trying to use historical arguments, isn't it true that in the 21st century in the United States of America—I mean here, before the Clone Wars—it was legal to kill unborn babies?"

"Well, yes, I suppose. But that was actually true in the 20th century. That was when the Supreme Court decided that a pregnant woman had a right to choose whether or not to have an abortion. It was actually the mid- to late-20th century—1973 AD to be exact."

"Well, then, isn't abortion the right thing to do? I mean, I thought the Supreme Court was made up of the wisest men and women. They can't be wrong, right? Maybe you are wrong."

"Well, Nova, first of all, the truth is the truth even if no one believes it. And furthermore, the Supreme Court was made up of only nine people. Do you want nine people to tell you what to do? Do you want nine people to tell a whole country what to do?"

Nova once again shifted her weight from one foot to the other. "I mean, but they are the wisest nine people. And isn't that what New America is proposing: that we have checks and balances on our new government? Aren't we going to create our new government based on the government of Old America?"

"You are conflating a lot of issues there. You can't impose a judicial decision on a social or political problem. But let's leave the branches-of-government argument for another time and focus on the issue of abortion. So are you saying the Supreme Court can't be wrong about legalizing abortion and having abortion government funded because the Supreme Court never made mistakes?"

Nova looked away from Hector and bit her lower lip. "I guess."

"So the Supreme Court of the United States also decided that Black people could never become citizens of their country. It was a seven-to-two decision—that would be what is called the Dred Scott decision. The court ruled that there was a 'perpetual and impassable barrier' between White and Black people. Much like the birth canal was considered a 'perpetual and impassable' barrier between a human baby and, I don't know, not a human baby, an undocumented human being, I guess you could say, right? Can you imagine that, one minute, you are in the birth canal and therefore not a human, with no right to life, and then literally one minute later you are considered a human citizen with all the rights therein. Silly and morally reprehensible. And the Dred Scott decision was also morally reprehensible. It basically legalized slavery in all the states. Thankfully, that decision was met with a huge backlash. As a matter of fact, that decision led to the Republican party getting its first elected President, Abraham Lincoln, and it led to the Civil War where approximately 700,000 men, the majority were White men mind you, died to free Black people from slavery. So, you see, you can have bad decisions made by the courts."

"So," Nova followed up, "you are saying that most people were against the Dred Scott decision at the time. But were most people against *Roe v. Wade* at the time?"

"Good question. According to polls, it was about 50/50. The funny thing is the majority of the abortion supporters also supported mass immigration on its southern borders. They didn't want to defend their southern border, many wanted open borders. But there was another southern border, if you will, that these same people defended strongly. Why didn't they apply their open border policy to the birth canal? So undocumented people can cross the border, but undocumented human babies could not cross THAT border. I mean, the birth certificate is the documentation needed for citizenship. And undocumented people have the right to cross borders and go through barriers, but undocumented babies who are trying to cross the border of the birth canal in hopes of a better life are stabbed, poisoned, crushed and dismembered. And the murder of these migrants is especially horrible because they are truly innocent, right, and they have no choice but to leave their homeland. They are truly forced to leave because the conditions where they used to live are no longer safe. I mean the argument that applies for immigrants applies to infants, too."

Nova took a deep breath. "I love you very deeply and I don't like to see you hurt. And I can tell this means a lot to you. But at the end of the day, I'm just really scared to go through with this."

Hector pointed to the dent on the front of his VTOL. "Have I ever shown you this dent?"

"Yeah, of course I've seen it before. You've had this old thing since before we met."

"But I never told you how I dented it."

"Yes, you did. You told me you hit a dog."

"I guess I should amend my comment. I meant to say, 'Have I ever told you the truth about how I got this dent?'"

Nova cocked her head questioningly and said nothing. Hector took a deep breath and continued, "It was not a dog. It was a beautiful 6-year-old girl."

"I never knew."

"But I did, and I live with it every day of my life. Not a day goes by that I don't think about what I did to that little girl and to her mother and father."

"But it was an accident. You did not do it on purpose."

"That doesn't matter. That is not important. I did five years for homicide without malice afore-thought. The state took five years of my life, but I took everything from that little girl's mother and father. I killed that girl and I will never forgive my-self. I don't want to kill another child."

Hector broke down in tears. Nova hugged him and consoled him. Her love and devotion to Hector won her heart and she vowed she would not go through with the abortion. She did not want to put him through that again. She would have the child and they would raise it together as husband and wife.

Later that day Nova whistled the sergeant of the Defense Team with her comscreen. When Trulia answered, Nova told her the good news. Trulia, in turn, whistled Preeta, who was taking a walk with

Simon. Preeta conveyed the good news to Simon that Nova was going to keep the baby.

"What made her change her mind?" Simon asked.

"A combination of things, I think. Trulia told me that she was taken aback by Hector drawing an analogy between abortion on the one hand and slavery and the Holocaust on the other. But mostly she just had a change of heart. Sometimes, men have that way with women, you know."

"For whatever reason she had a change of heart, that is wonderful news. Abortion is not only akin to slavery and the Holocaust, but the Anti-Y Movement post-Clone Wars."

Preeta answered back, "The Civil War is like the Clone Wars, but with the big difference that the right side won the Civil War while the wrong side won the Clone Wars. It is time for us to remedy that."

They walked back to the center of the city mostly in silence; Simon Peter had much to ponder. Finally, he asked what was on his mind: "What is New America's position on the death penalty? I mean, that you—that we—have respect for all life."

"We are taking a unique stance regarding capital punishment. There are two sides to that issue. Simply put, there are those who believe that nobody should be put to death. Period. They should just be imprisoned for life, so that they cannot harm other people again. And then there are those who believe in the death penalty for the most heinous murders and the most brutal and conscienceless murderers, and to merely give them a long term in prison is grossly disproportionate to the heinousness of the crime. The death penalty supporters would argue that studies show that it does in fact, act as a deterrent and therefore, does save lives. And then there is the idea of the death penalty as appropriate and proportional retribution. But then getting back to the other side of the argument, those against it say, in a nutshell, that we should heed the philosopher Nietzsche's warning; namely, that when fighting monsters, we must take care not to become monsters ourselves. 'Not in my name,' I guess they would say. They argue that if they participate in society by working, raising a family, voting, etcetera, then they are also committing murder behind the veneer of the state when any execution is performed. They do not want to be a part of that. Those were basically the issues that were debated."

"And so what is your unique solution?" Simon asked.

"That if someone is convicted of a brutal murder, the worst of the worst, then execution will only be allowed if an immediate family member is willing to pull the switch, so to speak—a husband, a wife, a mother, a father, an adult child, like that."

"So is that a compromise, in that families can still seek the ultimate punishment only if they are willing to retaliate themselves? That way, the individual citizen is not implicated. Is that it?"

"Yes, that is a good summary. We realize we are trying something novel, so we have placed a provision in our Constitution that we can change the law with only fifty percent of the general population electing to do so."

15

They arrived at the White House. Simon asserted his manhood in a respectful and gentlemanly manner. It was received passionately. He spontaneously took Preeta in his arms, cupped his hand over her cheek, pulled her to him and kissed her.

Preeta's guards had never been in this position before; they wanted to turn away, but they realized they could not avert their eyes from her because, after all, they were protecting her. The kiss lasted a long, long time. He pulled away, smiling at her with glazed eyes. With glazed eyes, she longed for more, but he stepped back and walked away toward home.

She watched him until he passed out of sight. She was late for her meeting.

A few weeks after that, Simon whistled her with his comscreen. Her 2D floating image appeared suspended in midair above the comscreen. He admired her image perhaps a bit too long before asking her on a date. She accepted. He asked her what her favorite type of food was. She answered East Indian. He invited her to his place, telling her he would prepare the best Indian food she had ever tasted.

Simon Peter made good on his promise. Over a dish of samosas with chutney, chickpea curry and naan bread, they enjoyed good music and good conversation.

Eventually, Preeta brought up the Love Factory. She calmly and straightforwardly told him that there were many governments in history that forbade their people things, yet hoarded them for themselves. For most of human history it had been this way—governments based on slavery, monarchies, theocracies. The only governments that had not engaged in this deprivation of their citizens were the ones based on free markets.

She used this as a springboard to talk about what the government of New America would be like. It would be fashioned after its namesake, the United States of America. She talked about the need for centralized governments; one could not have anarchy or tribalism. But she also mentioned that government should be limited in its power, and the best way to accomplish the goal of good government was to have innate checks and balances embedded within government itself. There would be different branches of government to help ensure that political authority did not become too powerful. She talked about ways of improving Old America's democracy by limiting political donations, not allowing lobbyists or corporate donations.

"We want to limit the power of corporations to influence our political organization," she concluded.

"You mean, Fidelity gets no more money from Sky Glass?" Simon joked.

"Sky Glass is the worst," said Preeta. "They give untold amounts to the Supreme Leader and the Central Committee in return for limited government regulation and for squashing competition. They also broadcast Fidelity's propaganda for her. It's a corrupt relationship."

"I don't even like the advertisements for the gladiator matches. I consider that propaganda because the government is giving credence to the whole madness of gladiator fights, and by extension the devaluing of the lives of men."

"Yes, and the movies they produce are full of indoctrination, too. Using stories as propaganda to brainwash the masses has been going on for centuries. I think there was a place in Old America that made it into an insidious art form. I think it was called Hollywood."

They talked well into the night. They talked politics. They talked morality and religion. He taught her everything he knew of the Bible and of Christian values. She received those ideas well. She thought to herself, *I like this Christianity; it explains why I feel about Simon the way I do. It's in harmony with my womanhood.* When they were done talking, they kissed. He asked her if this could officially be called a date. She gave him a positive response.

A few days later, they went on another date to the Mississippi River. This time they did not talk about anything serious. They swam in the river. They ate. They laughed together. And even though it made Preeta's guards uneasy, they gave each other massages.

On the way back to the White House, Preeta informed Simon that he needed to undergo training for his new leadership role. That training would include modern tactical warfare, fitness training, military history and modern political theory. Simon told her that he looked forward to the training, but he asked her yet again if this was a date or if this was business. She replied that it was a date but that, given the situation in the world, mixing business and pleasure was a necessity. She added, "But I do love you."

It was actually a Freudian slip; she did not mean to say it out loud, especially to him. She immediately followed it up with, "I'm sorry. I did not mean to say that. It just came out. I'm sorry. Don't feel that you need to..."

"Wait. Stop," urged Simon. They stopped walking. "We're both adults here. I did not think it would come out this way, but I might as well say it to you: I love you. I have been meaning to say it for some time, but I wanted the moment to be perfect..."

"Now you wait. Now you stop," Preeta told him. "The moment is perfect." They embraced and kissed. When they separated, she had a tear running down her cheek. Simon wiped it away with his finger and kissed her again. They smiled and gazed into each other's eyes for what seemed like an eternity.

16

The very next day, Simon began his training with the other freedom fighters. During this time, he took classes on political theory and history to gain an appreciation of the proposed political system for a liberated Pythia; he took military leadership classes to learn how to lead by example—in thought, word, and deed; he studied war fighting, which was conducted both in the classroom (tactical warfare and strategic planning through the ages) as well as practical application in the field through the use of firearms, stun guns, fighter drones, laser guns, shockwave guns, military robots, smart grenades, enhanced reality goggles, and more; and he underwent fitness, obstacle and combat training.

It was a rigorous schedule, yet Simon Peter rose to the occasion. Still, he could not quite think of himself as a leader. Yes, he told himself he was a good fighter and yes, he had a good moral compass, but that was a far cry from leading men and women into battle and into a more ethical and humane world order. *I am a gladiator. Now I must become a leader of people. As a leader, my success depends on the success of the people I am leading. I must change my perspective.* Simon took his lessons seriously and he prayed on it.

This training lasted many weeks. During the day, Simon worked hard, but in the evenings he looked forward to spending time with Preeta alone. (And for her part, Preeta found that she had more time now than ever before because, even though she had time-consuming obligations to keep New America running smoothly and to keep the revolution progressing smoothly, she no longer had to split her time at Delilah. She no longer had to waste her time at cabinet meetings and to carry the burden of pretense that she supported her mother, the subjugation of men, and the oppression of the state. Before the bold escape in which she helped bring Simon Peter to safety, one of her duties to her mother the Supreme Leader was to visit other precincts to boost morale and to negotiate on behalf of her mother. She used to use that duty as an opportunity to sneak away to New America. But now that burden was lifted, that pretense unnecessary, and she could spend her entire time working in New America.)

Almost every day, Simon would spend his lunches with the other freedom fighters. He befriended and grew close to Frank and Luna Lux, who were illegally married in a civil court of New America, and Sam Fing and Eppy Phinny, who were engaged to be married. They often discussed their training and the new form of government that was yet to be, that they hoped to play a hand in creating.

Frank immediately ruled out anything resembling socialism or fascism. "Socialism and fascism are one and the same—both are statism in which the government has strong centralized power, permitting no opposition or criticism, controlling all affairs of the nation."

"Surely, you can't be equating Hitler's Germany with Stalin's U.S.S.R.," Simon Peter responded.

"And why not?" Frank shot back. "Just think about it, what does Nazi stand for? National Socialist German Worker's Party." He raised his voice for emphasis when he said the word socialist. "Even Hitler said, 'There is more that binds us to Bolshevism than separates us from it.' And he meant it, too. Both countries had a common enemy: the principles of the free market, democracy and a republican form of government."

Eppy chimed in, "I am against fascism, for sure, but socialism/communism have a certain appeal to me. Even the root words are benevolent. Don't you like being social and communal over capital?"

"Fascism and communism seek to control the individual. The individual is subordinate to the state. Only with republican democracy tied in with a free market can you ever have the concept of individual rights and self-determination. In capitalism, property is privately owned, and the government's function is restricted to the protection of individual rights. In capitalism, the citizens not only have access to many goods and services, they live in a freer society. Individual autonomy is king. Historically, that is where women's rights came from. The freedom to be you. Now along with that is the freedom someone else has to invent an airplane, for instance. People work better, individually and communally, when they get to reap the benefits of their labor. Capitalism harnesses human nature and creates a system that potentially can benefit everyone."

Eppy leaned into Frank. "Potentially."

"Yes, 'potentially.' Government can only do so much. You can't turn to government for every little thing. Some problems are just endemic to humanity; government can't fix them. As long as we have an equal opportunity to live well, that is all we can expect from government. Sooner or later, we have to take responsibility for our own well-being. If the state takes care of you, then it becomes like your

Mommy or Daddy and historically it has always led to alcoholism and crime and just plain dysfunctional behavior."

"I would agree there," Sam chimed in. "Equality does not mean sameness."

Luna said, "Free market capitalism is natural and normal. It's the way humans naturally interact with each other. I voluntarily make something or perform some service and then I freely sell it to you. Your free will dictates your work, it is morally superior to any other economic system."

"But, no, see…that is where you are wrong," Eppy disputed. "We don't exercise our free will when we work. We have to work to eat and survive."

"Sure," said Luna. "But that is exactly the point that Frank and I are making here: That's just the way the world is. If you don't plant that crop, you won't eat. If you don't build a shelter, you will be exposed to the environment. If you don't sew new clothes, you will walk around naked."

"Hey, now, that sounds good to me," joked Frank.

"I'm being serious here. This is important. We don't want to throw Fidelity out of power and then just substitute another oppressive regime for the old one. We want something better. A limited government with checks and balances so that people can live as freely as we can in accordance with the rest of society."

"And are you saying that can only be the Old American model? Why can't it be socialism?" Simon Peter asked.

The rest of the table fell silent, stunned at what Simon had said. It was one thing for them to discuss the pros and cons of different governments, but Simon was to be the leader of the liberation. He had to be sure of himself.

Simon felt awkward, so he continued. "Look. I am in this fight to the end. I mean, if nothing else, I want to liberate men from our horrific condition. Don't worry, I am with you. But I am not as educated as the rest of you, and we should be able to discuss this openly."

Frank said, "We are not concerned. We know you are with us. But when we defeat Fidelity—and we will—we need to ensure a better living condition than has been in place for hundreds of years now. And to get back to your question, Simon, I will just say this: All throughout history, no socialist government has ever been successful; rather, they have been oppressive and are responsible for the genocide of over a hundred million people. I mean even if you take the Nazis out of the picture, the U.S.S.R. under Stalin killed over sixty million peasants, the Chinese communists under Mao alone killed forty-five million people. And then add Pol Pot with about two million. And add to that Ho Chi Minh and Castro and Che Guevara. It is upwards of a hundred million people."

Simon stood up; he wanted to put emphasis on his next statement. "I would add Cain to that list. Cain was the first murderous socialist. He killed his own brother Abel because he was jealous of his brother, and because his brother believed in God and worked and was more fruitful than he was. He wanted to 'redistribute' what was not his." Simon sat back down in his chair.

Sam chimed in for the first time, "And when God tried to tell Cain that the evil was in him and not in his brother, Cain was unable to comprehend that. Just like the socialists and the ruling class women of today who will not listen to the central tenet of Judeo-Christian teaching, that we fix the world by fixing ourselves, rather than remaking the world to fit our own broken selves and to placate our own desires."

Now Luna stood up from her chair. "Jealousy is a big part of the appeal of socialism and communism. Many people who want the redistribution of wealth realize that their well-being will be worse under socialism than with free enterprise, yet they advocate for redistribution because, even though they realize they will suffer under these reforms, they hope that the rich, whom they envy, will suffer even more."

Sam added, "To a communist, the greatest goal of a slave is not liberty, but to have a slave of his own. In a democratic republic with a free economy, however, a person realizes that to be free from someone else's control, you must relinquish control of your fellow citizens. Those prone to jealousy and who consider themselves victims are amenable to socialism, while those who like to be left alone to pursue their happiness lean towards private ownership instead of state ownership."

"But wait a minute," said Eppy. "Socialism has never really been tried."

"Oh, give me a break," said Frank. "That argument is literally hundreds of years old. The U.S.S.R. and Communist China were the living embodiment of socialist ideas. There is not a tenet in Marx's *Communist Manifesto* that was not applied in those countries. The misery and mass murder were not caused by 'not enough socialism,' but by too much socialism. It was not an absence of socialist principles but a consequence of them. And note that partial capitalism works better than partial socialism. When China and the Soviet Union adopted some free-market liberal reforms, the economy did not collapse, it strengthened. Everywhere you look throughout history, the less socialist the economy, the less poverty, the more prosperity, and far greater human rights protections. Capitalism has lifted countless millions out of poverty like no other system on Pythia, and has seen the explosion of inventions and cures for diseases."

"And I will say this," added Luna. "When America and Western Europe fell to the communists, that was the beginning of the Clone Wars and the devastation of men. And I love my man here, and I personally like men in my life."

"OK," concluded Eppy Phinny. "I think I am experiencing a revelation here. Let's fight for our freedom and for the liberation of mankind. We can work out our political and economic system later."

"Not to change the subject here, but I have a personal question to ask all of you. What are your thoughts on me asking Preeta for her hand in marriage?" Simon asked.

They all chimed in with positive feedback. "That would be a wonderful idea," was the general consensus at the table.

"But I feel so inadequate. I am just a man, after all. And only a gladiator. She is wise, erudite, a born leader. She is the leader of the liberation. She has way more important things on her mind than marriage."

"But she is also a woman," said Luna. "And the most important things in life are the seemingly unimportant, everyday things."

Sam put his arm around Simon. "And what are we fighting for anyway, man? You two are in a position of leadership and what better way to show how men and women can coexist equally than for you two to get married. Go for it, man."

17

A few weeks after that, Simon whistled Preeta with his comscreen. When she answered, he told her that he wanted to take her on a special date. He asked her out that night. They went shopping together, ate a five-course meal at the best restaurant in New America, and when they went back to his house and entered the doorway, they noticed a path of rose petals leading from the doorway to the bedroom. Inside the house, helium-filled red balloons with silver streamers hung from the ceiling, a cornucopia of chocolates and champagne lay on the kitchen table, and the bedroom was lavishly festooned with lighted candles, white towels on the bed folded into the shape of two swans kissing, and red rose petals spread on the bed in the shape of a Valentine's heart.

"And what is all this?" asked Preeta.

"Just a little touch-up I asked some friends from military school to do while we were out." Simon lowered himself to one knee.

"Oh…" Preeta put her hands to her mouth, then shook her hands in excitement, then put her hands to her mouth once again.

Simon pulled out an engagement ring. "Preeta Flake, will you make me the happiest man on Pythia and marry me? I promise to make you happy all of the days of our lives together."

Preeta hopped up and down like a little girl. She told Simon that she had been imagining this day all her life and that she wished she could make this moment last forever. And of course, she said yes.

She knelt down to him and they both fell to the ground and kissed. She got on top of him and began taking off her top. But Simon told her to stop, to wait until their wedding night.

"But it would be such a waste to let the romantic setting be for nothing." She got up, went to the bedroom and collapsed on the bed (with new satin sheets thanks to Frank, Luna, Sam and Eppy). He followed her into the bedroom, but stood at the door. "Come here, my future husband," she called.

Simon replied, "I'm committing myself to you and only you for the rest of my life, but we will wait until we have actually committed to ourselves in marriage. I love you and I always will. But sex does not equal love. Making love with you within marriage will not just be a physical thing, it will be a spiritual thing, too."

"But I am a woman and you are a man. It is only natural."

"Not everything natural is good. And we will still be a man and woman after our marriage."

"A man is half a person. A woman is half a person. But when they unite, they become whole."

"I feel whole right now."

"Sex is vital to marriage," said Preeta.

"And marriage is vital to sex," Simon responded.

Preeta stood up from the bed. "All right, then, future husband for life, we will wait until marriage. There will be no lovemaking during our engagement. Now let me speak to the people and announce our engagement."

"Yes, future wife."

Preeta kissed him on the lips and immediately called her council on her comscreen to assemble the people of New America in the city square for a special announcement.

Standing on the steps of her White House with Simon at her side, she announced their engagement using her drone mic. "Thank you for gathering here on such short notice. In the past, I have used this venue to speak about urgent things that affected us all as a society, but now I wish to take up your time with something personal. I hope you don't mind. So now, without any ado, I am most happy to announce my engagement to my future husband, Simon Peter." The crowd applauded uproariously.

Simon leaned into her and whispered in her ear, "Now our love is extroverted."

Preeta laughed. She continued to the audience, "I have directed my council members and my personal team to make preparations for our wedding. We will be married tomorrow at two PM. All are welcome to celebrate this special and most joyous occasion."

Simon Peter was dumbstruck. *Marriage tomorrow? I was expecting a much longer engagement.* Preeta whispered in his ear, "You see, I am saving myself for marriage." She smiled, kissed him on the lips and walked back into the White House to begin preparations for the next day's ceremony.

The wedding and the reception afterwards were lovely, of course. The ceremony took place in the city chapel and the reception was held in the city square, the largest gathering place in New America. It was a traditional ceremony in the custom of a Christian wedding; that is, there were Christian prayers, there were readings from the Bible and there was an exchange of vows. Many of the customs, however, had to be heavily researched in just one night because weddings of any type were extremely rare. One of the history teachers took on the role of the officiant. Having studied Christianity and having read the

Bible, she was the most prepared in New America to take on the role.

The wedding itself was an act of dissent. Because human cloning was the main method of procreation, marriage had been outlawed. It was the Department of Religion's task to make certain men and women did not intermarry. Married women were fined and "re-educated" while men were imprisoned or even killed. There were to be no exceptions to the non-marriage rule, not even for the wealthy women who frequented Area 54. Such was the power of the state. Such is the ability of the majority to subjugate the minority.

All throughout history, governments have sought to separate people, including but not limited to followers of different religions, people of different ethnic groups, heterosexuals versus homosexuals, etcetera. The list goes on and on. And it is not that the state has created these divisions; rather, it is that the state has profited and prospered by dividing before conquering. This division finally culminated in the disenfranchisement of half the human population—men.

The state had a vested interest in keeping men subjugated and having women rule. But even women were growing weary of the exploitation of men. It might even be said that a majority of the common women wanted to live freely with men in an egalitarian society. They just needed to unite, which was difficult considering that the governments of Pythia controlled assembly, speech, and media.

The weight of oppression would surely cause the collapse of this draconian world order sooner or later. Hopefully, with the leadership of Simon Peter, it would be sooner rather than later.

That was precisely why this wedding was so important to so many freedom fighters. It was seen as the dawn of a new beginning, one of hope that men and women could coexist freely and openly. And that was precisely why, when there was any mention of God in the ceremony, the guests cheered and clapped, especially when Simon Peter got to the part in his vows, "…according to God's holy ordinance."

After the exchange of vows and of wedding rings, and the closing prayer, the officiant finally said, "You may now kiss the bride."

The officiant then turned to the guests and said, "It is now my privilege to introduce to you for the first time Mr. and Mrs.—" She paused. During this awkward moment of silence, both Simon and Preeta turned to the officiant. She whispered to them, "Is it 'Mr. and Mrs. Flake,' or is it 'Mr. and Mrs. Peter,' which is really a first name—men have no family names?"

"We'll figure that one out later," said Preeta.

"I guess that was one detail we forgot in the rush," said Simon.

Preeta turned round to the guests, held her hands in the air in victory and proclaimed, "We're married. Let's go celebrate."

The reception was magnificent. Even though they had less than a day to plan the ceremony and reception, almost all of the townspeople contributed and many hands make light work. The partying and the feasting lasted well into the wee hours of the night—into the early morning hours of the next day, really—but very early in the evening, Preeta turned to Simon, kissed him on his cheek and in a low voice, said, "We're married. Let's go celebrate."

He looked at her. She looked at once demure yet aggressive. It was clearly an advance, and how, at this point, could Simon Peter deny her? After all they were, in fact, now very much married. They left the revelers for Preeta's house.

As they entered her bedroom, Simon could not take his eyes off her. As she talked, his gaze rested on her lower lip as if lip reading. She noticed this. They embraced. For the first time in both their lives, they were making love.

She had had sex before. It was expected of women to sow their wild oats. He too, had had many sexual encounters. That was considered a reward for winning a fight, and many women paid dearly to be with a gladiator. There had been many women, but he'd never felt emotion.

Sex is so much more than sex. Many might say that to extricate feelings from sex is liberating, but in reality it is disingenuous, and disconnecting love from sex has hurt human beings. Simon and Preeta restored the sexual experience as a simultaneous physical, emotional and spiritual activity that forms deep emotional bonds between two lovers. As the mattress sang its creaky song, the two fell apart, shaking, spent. They had consummated their marriage. It was a rebellious act.

18

The next morning should have been a quiet moment, two young newlyweds basking in their afterglow, but it was not to be. The whole town was awakened by bombs exploding above ground and by blasts from shockwave launchers from above, causing tremendous reverberations down below in New America. The limestone ceilings were collapsing onto the underground city, damaging the buildings. The sub-floor of New America quaked and convulsed, and the noise within the subterranean city was thunderous, exacerbated by the sirens blaring to give warning, but it was too late for warnings now.

The blast knocked Preeta flat against the ground, the shockwave rolling over her like an ocean under-tow breaking overhead, with bits of debris falling on top of her and around her. She bounced back to her feet and through the ringing in her ears, she heard her husband yell for his comscreen and defense console. Preeta's guards crashed into the room, handing Simon the tools he would need to lead the defense of New America. His training would now be tested in a real conflict.

The men and women quickly went to their battle stations. When the Supreme Forces are your enemy, every citizen must be armed and every citizen must be able to defend the city.

Inexplicably, the elevator platforms began to descend. They were exposed. Bullets, proton torpedo launchers, and laser cannons came flying into the cavernous sanctuary of New America in one fell swoop. The sheer unexpectedness of the attack nearly cost the citizens their lives, but the people were prepared and at the ready with their defenses, awaiting orders from their military leader.

Simon ordered into his comscreen, "Above ground sector line: jam all transmissions. I repeat, jam all transmissions."

It was too late; they were being strafed with laser fire that turned buildings into clouds of atomized shrapnel. The firepower was coming from a haunt-ingly large airship that was hovering above them. The aircraft was over the opening to New America and spanned an area larger than the opening itself. It was an ominous sight, blocking out the sun and equally ominous because it was silent; there were no engines to be heard and no thrust to be seen.

Savy Noir entered the room. "The Supreme Forces must have known we were here. How can that be?"

Simon Peter ignored her. "All sectors: Deploy anti-aircraft proton torpedoes."

Even though the sensors and cameras had taken a beating from the Supreme Forces' onslaught, Simon could see on his defense console something that was unimaginable. No technology of which Simon was aware could explain what he saw. It was like sorcery.

The image that appeared on his console was dark, grainy, and badly pixelated, yet it was unmistakable. The women of the Supreme Forces, accompanied by military robots, were walking from the colossal hovering machine down to the surface of Pythia and even making their way directly into the bed of New America.

He showed the rest of his team. It gave the impression that the troopers and the humanoid fighting bots were taking steps, as if walking on the ground, only there was nothing visible. They were walking on air!

Savy's jaw dropped. "Holy Sanger! It's a worm corridor! Fidelity mentioned it to me in passing, and I spoke about it with Saridian, but I thought this was in the developmental stage, in its infancy. More science fiction than scientific reality."

"How is it possible? What's the technology?" asked Preeta.

"Not sure. I think it has something to do with sound frequencies resonating with the atmosphere such that the air molecules vibrate synchronously, creating a sort of tunnel."

"You mean, they can literally walk on air?" Preeta was amazed; Fidelity had not made her privy to the worm corridor experiments.

"That means we can walk on air, too," exclaimed Preeta.

Simon ordered into his comscreen, "Turn off all sirens."

They could hear the humming of the worm corridor, supporting Savy's theory.

Simon Peter said that he had a better idea. "Bring me my Gogs and get the entire fleet of fighter drones and mosquito drones ready."

The woman on the other end of the comscreen bellowed back, "Copy that. Affirmative."

Savy asked, "What are you doing? We need to arm our infantry with exoskeletons and firepower and go above ground and defend our city."

"Not with that cover, we're not. That is precisely what they are expecting. We would lose too many lives. I have a better plan. That is a tokamak fusion-powered flying warcraft, is it not?"

Upon receiving his enhanced reality goggles, Simon immediately went into action. Preeta and Savy dashed out of the room to the armory, donned their exoskeletons and weapons, and ran to the center of town, just below the opening. Preeta dove to the side, narrowly dodging a salvo of bullets that dotted the cavern floor. Savy evaded a laser bolt and fired back at the incoming troops, striking an attacker. She fired again, and another foe went the way of the first.

"What is Simon planning?" Savy asked Preeta.

"I don't know. Some kind of sabotage, I suppose."

Back in Preeta's room, Simon guided his squad of drones with his goggles. They flew up the worm corridor like salmon spawning upriver, with the fighter drones providing cover for the mosquito drones. *It only takes one mosquito*, he thought as he guided the lone flyer into the bowels of the ship.

The freedom fighters looked up at the hostile warplane and saw a large black and white plume of vapor escape out of the rear like an active volcano. The freedom fighters witnessed the collapse of the worm corridor, and the female combatants and military bots free-falling to their deaths and destruction. They also noted the silence, as the attack ceased.

"Simon's sabotage of the ship worked," exclaimed Preeta.

All of the freedom fighters cheered wildly. They had suffered relatively minor casualties, while

Fidelity's women suffered great loss of life. This was clearly a victory for the liberation.

Simon ran out to the square, comscreen still in hand.

"What did you do?" asked Savy.

"Fusion is a process that liberates a remarkable amount of heat and energy. That heat must be controlled. I merely guided my one lovely drone into the engine room and severed the coolant reservoir. Voila. Disabled ship."

"But won't the ship blow?"

"They have time to escape. They can make their way back to their base and shut off the engines long before that happens."

But while all the citizens looked up at the warship, it was apparent that it wasn't moving anywhere and equally apparent that it was overheating.

"Close the elevator platform," ordered Simon into his comscreen. "I repeat, close the elevator platform."

The elevator platform sealed off the surface not a moment too soon. Fidelity's grandest flying weapon exploded, killing the crew inside. Clearly Fidelity had decided to eschew escape in favor of revenge.

In the aftermath of their successful defense, during the cleanup and the inspection for damage, Simon Peter approached Preeta to ask her to convey a message to her mother. Simon wanted Fidelity to know that he was willing to give the bodies of the fallen Supreme Forces to the state so that the women could be given a proper burial. "We are not savages, after all," he concluded.

The message was sent. Fidelity agreed. New America flew in transport planes with about 150 caskets. The planes landed just outside the gates of the Supreme Compound. The gates opened. The women of the Unified Governments, with the aid of the men and women of New America, brought the caskets into the compound. Fidelity stood atop the compound wall and gazed at Simon Peter with acrimony.

He used his drone microphone to say to her, "We are not savages, after all."

The gates closed.

Night fell.

The men and women of the liberation burst out of the caskets like Spartan warriors entering Troy. Clearly Simon Peter knew his Greek mythology.

PART
FIVE

19

John John was one of the men and women hiding in the caskets. He was the leader of this mission, the goal of which was to capture Fidelity and nullify her stronghold on the women-folk. The team of 150 men and women made their way to the Central Committee Chambers, the entrance to Fidelity's personal quarters. Under the dark of night, they met no resistance until they reached the steps of the chambers and encountered Fidelity's personal bodyguards.

"Stop. Who goes there?" one of the bodyguards called.

"You need to get out of our way, we have a job to do," replied John John.

"Keep your hands where we can see them, or else we will shoot to kill," was the only response from the bodyguard.

"You will have to kill me to stop me," warned John John.

True to her word, the bodyguard pulled her laser pistol from its holster and aimed it straight at John John. But one of the liberators got to her first. The laser bolt caught the bodyguard dead center, and her body turned into a turmoil of flame and sparks and settled into an ooze of acrid smoke. As other bodyguards assembled at the top of the stairs, one of them called out, "We're just doing our duty."

John John reached for his laser gun. "You still have the option of getting out of our way."

"That's no option," came the reply.

"I will give you until the count of ten to put your weapons down and get out of our way," said John John as he and the rest of the liberators pointed their weapons at the guards. One...two...three... four...five...six...seven..." He commenced firing at the count of seven.

This was the head start that made all the difference. It caught the bodyguards off balance. The laser guns were on repeater mode and hitting their marks with precision, blasting into the guards and into the walls behind them, leaving in their wake molten shards and reflected light. It helped that the bodyguards were outnumbered by the freedom fighters and, for the next couple of heartbeats, essentially blinded by the reflected light. A couple of heartbeats was all John John needed to enter the building. Now the task was to find Fidelity's personal chambers, and this would be no easy task in the labyrinthine interior.

Even though the fight with the bodyguards hadn't taken long and was reasonably quiet, Fidelity knew of the liberators' incursion. One of the bodyguards must have been able to comchat with the rest of the security force during the initial encounter with John John and his team. Fidelity sank to a new low. She ordered her security team to assemble dozens of children in and around her personal chambers to act as a human shield.

When John John and his team saw the children who ranged in age from four to thirteen—including babies in the arms of older children—he immediately ordered a halt. He took out his comchat and spoke to Simon Peter directly, informing him of this new revelation and asking for further instructions.

Simon Peter was stunned by the news. Even he found it difficult to process how snake-like Fidelity could be. "Damn it to Sanger. Yes, of course, you are right. Retreat. Assemble your team around the perimeter of the chambers. Don't let anyone in or out."

"Copy that," said John John. "We have the situation under control. I will send some liberators to open the gates."

"Copy that. Reinforcements on the way."

As the small group of liberators made their way from the Central Committee Chambers to the gates of the compound, they saw Fidelity's soldiers rousing young children from their homes. Babies were crying in their older sisters' arms, and little girls were still in their pajamas, holding dolls and teddy bears, filling the streets. When the gates were opened and Simon Peter and his reinforcements entered the compound, it was a surreal experience.

Simon felt disoriented, as if he was experiencing the hallucinatory quality of a dream. The children seemed to be moving in slow motion. Even though he scanned the streets quickly, turning his head fast from left to right, he processed the visual information in slow motion. He knew, however, that he had to shed this feeling, that he had to come back fully to reality.

He was shocked out of his dreamlike sequence by Fidelity's Sky Force. A large shadow, created by Sky Base blocking out the sun, cast itself on the compound. Out of Sky Base, one of the state's many airborne aircraft carriers, came the dreaded Chameleon Fighters, so called not only because they could camouflage themselves using cameras and mirrors, but for their flying abilities. They had both front and rear thrusters so that they could easily fly forward and back, much like the gait of a chameleon.

As a child, Simon Peter used to watch Fidelity's Chameleon Fighters performing practice maneuvers and he noted that the planes seemed to move back and forth like a pendulum, or even like a tod-dler's toy truck scooting back and forth on the floor. These fighters were used mainly for strafing enemy territory. Their maneuverability was unmatched by any fighter plane in history.

Seven Chameleons ejected from Sky Base and sprayed the grounds of the compound with invisi-ble photons of light, attacking indiscriminately and killing men, women and the innocent children, who had just been roused from their sleep. Swoop. Swoop. Swoop. Left. Right. Front. Back. Leaving death and destruction in their path.

There was nothing Simon Peter or the rest of the liberation could do. They had not prepared for this; they thought theirs was a surprise attack. They had expected Fidelity's ground troops, but not an airstrike.

How could Fidelity have called up Sky Force so quickly? Simon did all he could: He summoned his men to triage the fallen. And then, just as quickly as it started, the Chameleons retreated back into Sky Base like bees returning to their hive. And just as Sky Base had suddenly filled the skies, so too did it withdraw, leaving only peaceful blue skies and white clouds, belying the death and destruction that it had unleashed on the compound.

Fidelity's Female Force (the FFF) came out of their posts and helped with the triage of the air-strike victims. They aided not only the women and the children, who were almost exclusively girls, but the men as well. Saridian Ventue, Secretary of War, approached Simon Peter and told him that she was in charge of a large contingency of the FFF who had defected from the state and vowed their loyalty to the freedom fighters. They did so out of disgust that Fidelity would use children as a human shield and in response to her utter disregard for their welfare by using Sky Force to attack the compound.

If Fidelity's self-preservation at the expense of all other considerations had not been clear before, it was certainly clear now. Even though her regime had prospered for years, there were many women who dissented. But there was no recourse, they'd had no options. At least not until Simon Peter and the rest of the revolutionary fighters had risen up. Now the dissenting women had a choice, and hope for a brighter future.

"For the first time in too many years, women will stand by men, as equals," Saridian summarized.

Simon Peter smiled and using his drone mic, called out towards the Central Chambers, "Fidelity, you are losing your support. Your very own Secretary of War, along with most of the FFF, have abandoned you. Give yourself up and you will not be harmed. You have my word."

There was no answer.

But at that moment, John John called Simon on his comscreen. "We need to talk. Privately. Can we meet at the Central Bank by the recycling plant?"

20

The Supreme Compound was constructed such that the Central Committee Chambers was at the very center of the gated city, set up like a panopticon so that Fidelity could see into every building. As Simon walked up the steps to the Central Bank, he had an eerie feeling that Fidelity was watching him. After all, she was still inside the Central Chambers. Simon watched a garbage truck enter the recycling plant, which was the next building over.

Are Fidelity's die hard minions hiding in the garbage truck, ready to pounce at me? thought Simon. No, the bots were just collecting garbage. *I suppose garbage has to be collected and recycled even when you are being attacked by freedom fighters. But then again, the robots are programmed to collect at this time, regardless of the circumstances.*

When Simon entered the bank, John John was there waiting for him. John John spoke first. "I have betrayed you. I have betrayed the movement. I deserve to die."

Simon was incredulous. "What, pray tell, could you possibly be talking about?"

"I have harmed the cause. I deserve to die," John John repeated stoically.

"Explain yourself, man." Simon grew impatient.

"I am responsible for the Sky Force attack. I ordered a contingent of our fighters to commandeer an airborne aircraft carrier, and I myself programmed the military robots to sweep the compound with tactical high-energy lasers."

"But why? Why would you do such a thing?"

"I wanted the women to think that Fidelity's troops were behind the attack. I wanted her troops to abandon her. It was a propaganda tool. And it worked, but you have to believe me when I say that I did not know that there would be children on the grounds. I imagined only her troops on the ground. I guess I expected children and ordinary citizens would be asleep safely in their quarters."

Simon thought through the ramifications of what he had just heard. "This changes everything. I must go out and tell the women that it was us who led the attack, not Fidelity."

"No, you cannot do that. I am responsible, and I take full responsibility, but the good fight must go on."

"Not like this. I must tell them the truth. If we want to live in harmony, we must be honest with them. That is the only way."

"No, I beg you. It is all my fault. I don't deserve to live. I am not worthy to go on. I am not worthy to witness the fruits of our revolution. But you, my friend, must continue to fight for our freedom and equality."

John John took out a 9mm pistol, archaic yet deadly nonetheless, and handed it to Simon. "Here," he continued, "end my life now so that you can go on. I am the guilty one. You have done nothing. And don't punish the rest of the men who deserve to walk in freedom with the security of justice. Don't punish the women who know that their destiny is tied with ours. They need you, Simon. Please, kill me. Please, please...kill me."

"You're crazy." Simon let the handgun drop to the floor and turned to walk out the door. "I will tell the people now." He walked briskly down the stairs, heading towards the triage sites where most of Fidelity's fighters would be congregated.

John John ran past him down the stairs and hurled himself into a garbage truck, to be ground up by the truck's auger like so much rubbish.

Impressions ran through Simon Peter's mind like flickering photos in a zoetrope, each idea competing for supremacy. *What did I just witness? John John, suicide. He must have been despondent. I could've helped him. He betrayed me. He betrayed the cause. I must tend to the women. They have been betrayed. I have lost my best friend.* His imaginings were competing for dominance, but one concept won out: He must inform the people that it was not Sky Force, but rather his freedom fighters who had sabotaged Fidelity's fleet.

As he walked to the Chambers intent on exposing the truth behind the attacks, he did not think about what he was going to say. He would just be honest and forthright with the group and did not prepare any type of speech. Time was of the essence and he was keenly aware that the fight with Fidelity and the powers that be was not anywhere near over.

Simon's decision to just come out with the bald truth freed up his mind to speculate on John John and his disloyalty. *It took years to build up our trust in each other, but it took only one brief moment to break that bond. I would've taken a bullet for that man; it ended up that he was the one who pulled the proverbial trigger and shot me.*

When he found himself on the steps of the Central Committee Chambers, he used a drone mic and announced straight-forwardly, "Attention, everyone. May I have your attention? It was not Fidelity who planned the air strike, it was my lieutenant. It was us."

He let that sink in. He knew he had gotten their attention because they stopped talking with each other and even paused their work. Upon hearing the news, Preeta and Savy ran to the top of the steps.

"Is this true?" demanded Savy.

"Yes, of course it is true," replied Simon. "I certainly would not announce it otherwise."

"But how do you know?" she pressed.

"John John told me he planned it. He hatched the whole plot himself, using his own team to carry it out."

"This is terrible news. We will deal with John John at a later date, we have more pressing concerns now."

With a lump in his throat, holding back tears, Simon Peter said, "John John has already been dealt with."

Preeta chimed in, "But even so, you cannot undermine our whole effort just because of one bad apple. You should've at least discussed it with us first before presenting it to the masses."

"We will be triumphant," asserted Simon Peter. "The revolution will succeed. Men and women will live in freedom and prosperity, able to pursue happiness together as one. But we must be honest with them from the very beginning, starting now. We have an opportunity to create a solid foundation. We should not fail so early on."

A woman from the crowd wearing a black beret, with a stethoscope around her neck shouted, "Why should we be on your side? You're no better than women."

Simon advanced to the edge of the steps. "I am not asking you to be on our side. You should never be on people's sides, because all people are flawed and prone to wrong-thinking. You should always side with truth, justice, mercy and faithfulness."

"Did you hear that, ladies?" said the woman. "This man wants us to side with the truth, while he has been hiding the truth from us. He betrayed us. We changed sides because we thought Fidelity had attacked innocent children and civilians, but it was really Simon Peter and his ilk."

Preeta stepped up to Simon's drone mic and called out to the women, "No. Didn't you hear what he said? It was not him. It was one of his lieutenants, yes, but Simon Peter was not aware of it. I can personally vouch for him. He is a good man. He would never condone such a thing. And look at what he is doing here: As soon as he found out, he wasted no time and immediately told all of you. He did not even seek our advice. He knew what to do; his conscience told him the right thing to do." Preeta put her hand on Simon's shoulder. "This man is trying to make it right."

"That's right, ladies," the woman with the stethoscope said. "This MAN is trying to make it right. As soon as we put our trust in men, we are betrayed."

"What are you saying?" asked Preeta. "Are you really saying that only women can be trusted to treat women fairly? Please reconsider. That is foolishness. So only White people can be trusted to treat White people fairly? Only Black people can be trusted to treat Black people fairly? History has shown time after time that that is false. Gender solidarity is a lie."

Simon Peter followed suit, "I can assure you that I had no knowledge of the attack, yet I can see your position. You do not know us. We men have not been in a position of power and you fear the unknown. I get that. But let me offer you this: Fight with us. Let's defeat our common enemy, Fidelity and her state-run oppression. After we have liberated men and the women who love them, we will create two states. You can elect your own leaders, you can be free to express yourselves, have freedom of speech and assembly, you can govern yourselves and you can arm yourselves to protect against tyranny..."

21

"So generous of you, giving women what they already have," spat Fidelity, emerging from the Chamber doors, surrounded by little girls for protection.

Simon Peter ignored her gibe and addressed the most salient issue. "Let the children go. I promise that you will be unharmed."

Fidelity looked down at one of the girls and signaled to her with an almost imperceptible nod. The girl immediately began a diatribe against Simon Peter and men in general.

"How dare you? How dare you challenge Fidelity? How dare you abandon Fidelity? How dare you side with second-class citizens, men? How dare you?

After all Fidelity has done for you. After all she's given you. After all she has done to protect you."

Savy was not taken in by the plaintive call of the child. Rather, she saw through the sham: "Using children as verbal human shields who haven't developed the critical faculty required to synthesize complex ideas, let alone have the life experiences to speak with authority, is just disgusting. Have some decency. Using children to be your spokespeople is child abuse."

"Ha," Fidelity responded. "These children are speaking freely. Aren't you, my comrades?"

When the girls responded in the affirmative, Fidelity asked another girl to "educate the adults."

The girl screamed hysterically, "You have no right to treat Fidelity this way. Through her leadership, we are progressing towards world peace. Pythia will surely be a better place without men. We are getting close to losing our status as women—and it will all be your fault. Do you want to be on the wrong side of history? Well, you will be if you side with the weaker sex. We are at risk of extinction and all you can talk about is fairy tales of equality with men? Wake up. Wake up now before it is too late."

Simon Peter interjected, "Fidelity, these children have been brainwashed. They are doing your bidding, reciting your talking points on your behalf. I agree with Savi that this is a form of child abuse. You need to fight with the baby carriages behind you, not in front of you."

Fidelity confidently addressed the crowd. "Look at him. Pathetic liar, like all men. Pathetic. Can't be trusted. If I let the girls go, the first thing he will do is shoot me dead."

"Let the girls go," yelled the woman in the black beret.

Other women followed suit. One yelled, "You are using these children, treating them like disposable pawns in your game for political power."

Another exclaimed, "When you hide behind children, what you are really saying is that you can't make reasonable arguments and come up with solutions of your own like adults do."

Clearly, Fidelity had miscalculated her level of support. "Girls, you may go down the steps. Go now. Go. Go. Go." The girls hurried away. Fidelity pulled back her regal purple wrap to expose a 9mm pistol holstered on her hip.

Savy said there was no need for the weapon, and Fidelity responded, "We will see about that." She called out to the people, "We will see if men can be trusted. You will learn that they cannot. Once they take power, you women will once again become second-class citizens. No woman alive today is old enough to remember the days that women could not vote, women could not earn their own living, women were dependent upon men, women could not run for office, women were not educated. The list goes on. Do you want to go back to those days, comrades?"

Simon Peter sent a drone mic over to Fidelity. Using it, she repeated herself using almost the same words as a moment earlier, ending with the same query, that was certainly not meant to be rhetorical in nature: "Do you want to go back to those days, comrades?"

Preeta countered, "You mean the way men are treated today? Just because the past was bad, that doesn't mean you should make the present bad."

"Oh, my...she speaks. The traitor speaks. You've been more trouble to me than you're worth. I always suspected you loved men. You man lover, you. I grew deeply suspicious after the men escaped and you carried on as if nothing happened. You did not even mention their escape to me, not once. We never discussed it. That was when I had you followed. I discovered that when you were allegedly on your diplomatic excursions for the United Governments of Sanger, that you were really going into the No-Go Zone. After that, it was easy to figure out that it was the base for the rebellion."

"So that is how you discovered New America," said Savy. "I thought as much."

Fidelity began a chant, traditionally popular in Sanger: "Women hold up all the sky. Women hold up all the sky."

But no one chanted in return. Some of the women were actually vicariously embarrassed for Fidelity; it was as if she had egg on her face.

In desperation, Fidelity quickly changed tactics. "Women of Sanger, we have the right to rule. The law is on your side. Do not relinquish that for false promises, especially false promises made by the weaker sex."

Simon Peter addressed the crowd. "It is not a matter of having the right; rather, it is about being right."

Fidelity smirked and said, "Women hold up all the sky. We had been oppressed for millennia; now it is our turn."

"Your turn to what? Oppress?" Simon shot back.

"Women of the world, unite. Men are evil. Men will subjugate you. History has proven me correct."

"You create false enemies so that you can play the role of the hero. You are a self-manufactured 'hero.' Yes historically, before the Clone Wars, I will concede women were second-class citizens all over the planet. But that was not so much caused by men as by the harshness of existence. I mean, life was hard before modern times. Men had to do the hunting, men had to fight the battles, men did the heavy labor. As a consequence of the harshness of life, women were relegated to the rearing of children, the gathering of food, obtaining water for the village, and the like. But as technology advanced and things got easier for both men AND women, surely women obtained more rights and equity with men. At the end of the day, in a nutshell, men have always wanted to protect and care for women. The advent of modernity has led women to protest for equal rights, and for men to share those rights. But don't blame men for the harshness of life."

"Any student of history will tell you that it was men—men—who have started all wars." Fidelity felt assured that this would win over the women-folk.

Savi stepped up to the mic. "As Secretary of State, I can tell you that is simply not true. Throughout history, queens have been more likely to wage war than kings, and to acquire more territory than kings. Queen Isabella, Catherine the Great, and other women like Margaret Thatcher and Golda Meir and Indira Gandhi and countless other women, most notably Afifa Omar, after the Clone Wars."

"Well, of course, after the Clone Wars. We women rule now, so it stands to reason that women would be in positions to wage war," Fidelity said drolly.

"So that should show you that war is not waged by men, but by people in power," Savi retorted. "And we should also remember that no matter if it was a man or a woman who waged war, up until the Clone Wars, it was always men who were sent off to battle and who suffered a vast majority of the casualties and the violent deaths. When confronted with violent, aggressive and dangerous international situations, it was largely men who paid the price and made the ultimate sacrifice. And men should be given credit for ending wars, too."

"Ridiculous. I have never heard anything so preposterous. You are merely deflecting. Look at the air strike on innocent citizens and children—that was conducted by none other than a man. See, women, what men do?"

"That was not me, that was another man. Don't blame all men for what one man has done." Simon turned to the people at the bottom of the steps and in the courtyard. "But let's have the women decide. Let us vote on who should lead. Let us vote on which direction we should take as a society. On the one hand, more oppression and subjugation under Fidelity; or with us, where men and women will be equal and where we can pursue our own happiness freely."

"Nonsense. You wish to vote only because you are keenly aware that you will lose the battle. You cannot fight against the status quo," Fidelity sneered.

"I only wish to spare more bloodshed."

"Voting is for the weak. Democracies always fail because people are not able to manage themselves."

Savi cut her off. "I say we take a vote. Right here, right now. If the people want to continue with the status quo, with Fidelity as leader, we will leave quietly and return to New America. If the people want new leadership and a government by the people and for the people—all people, all races, religions, and men, too—then you and your forces must leave."

Fidelity responded, "Are you really that naive? Do you think for a moment that I believe you would just leave like that? Or that I would allow you to exist, in New America or elsewhere? And on the other hand, are you so stupid to believe that I would just walk away from what I have built? I have sacrificed much too much to become Supreme Leader and I will not surrender it freely, especially to men."

Preeta addressed the crowd. "What do you think? A vote once and for all to settle this in a non-violent way?"

The crowd cheered its approval.

Preeta entreated the crowd, "Let me hear a round of applause for Fidelity and her leadership."

The people shuffled their feet, looked around them, but there was total silence save for a cough or two and a baby crying.

Preeta then called for a vote. "Let me hear a round of applause for Simon Peter and his leadership."

The noise was deafening. Simon tried to tell the crowd that he was not the de facto leader of the rebellion, that the people could have a true and open election and elect their new leader at a later date, but the applause, the stamping of feet, the hooting and hollering made it impossible for him to be heard. A group of women climbed the steps to be with Simon and Preeta and Savi, leaving Fidelity forgotten in the background. The women cheered, the crowd was in a euphoric frenzy, anticipating a new dawn for humanity.

Just then a shot rang out. Fidelity had taken out her pistol and shot Savi, who collapsed to the ground. Fidelity pointed her weapon at the woman with the black beret and the stethoscope around her neck, but Simon Peter jumped in front of her to block the bullet. He succeeded. He took the bullet and collapsed.

Preeta leapt to Simon's side as he lay on the ground. Some of the women tended to Savi, and others came to Simon and Preeta's aid, while yet another group turned on Fidelity. But as they were approaching her, she grabbed a woman, spun her around, and pointed the gun at her head.

The women backed off. They did not want to light a fuse and ignite Fidelity's rage.

"Now, comrades," Fidelity hissed, "you will back off and let me walk out of here. This will not be the last you see…"

Preeta shot Fidelity with a laser. The former Supreme Leader was not the only one carrying a weapon. After all, only moments before, they had been in a heated battle. The beam hit its mark, piercing Fidelity's head and killing her instantly.

The hostage ran to the safety of the crowd, distraught. She turned, looked at the fallen body that was once Fidelity and began to chant, "She is not a woman. She is not a woman." The whole crowd of spectators, mostly women but men, too, joined in the chant.

Preeta wept over Simon's fallen body, but noticed his shallow breathing. He was not dead. They transported him to the hospital. His doctors told him that he would survive. He had lost a lot of blood and was very weakened, but he would make it.

Thank God, he thought. *I am not ready to leave Preeta. I am not ready to abandon the people in the dawn of liberty.*

22

On Simon Peter's last day on Earth (yes, the name had been changed back to Earth), Preeta came to the hospital to visit him. She asked him how he was doing and he said that, physically, the doctors told him he would live. He was happy about that, and elated, too, that the revolution had succeeded, that Fidelity and her oppressive government had been overthrown and that now men and women could live equally and freely. He was dispirited, however, at the loss of life on both sides of the fight.

In particular, he was disheartened by Savi Noir's demise. He blamed himself. He doubted himself. He confided in Preeta that maybe his values were all wrong. That maybe, just maybe, Savi died and he was shot because he was being punished for his beliefs and for his values.

Maybe he was wrong about everything he thought. Everybody goes through periods in their lives when they doubt themselves. This was that moment for Simon. Maybe he was wrong about his belief in America, maybe he was wrong to fight for a republican democracy, maybe he was wrong to fight for a free-market economy, wrong about socialism, wrong about his position on abortion.

Preeta tried to comfort him, but Simon could not be comforted. He told her that through all the doubt, he was always certain of two things: his undying love and devotion to her, and his faith in Jesus. He verbalized his love for her. "I love you," he said.

"You don't have to say it," she replied.

"Not expressing my love for you is like wrapping up a gift and then throwing it away. I think I was wrong about many things. There are always two ways to see every story. You can always tell one story from many different points of view."

"You can change the narrative, but you can't change the reality; you can change the fiction, but you can't change the basic truth."

"But what good is the narrative if it does not reflect reality."

"Oh Simon, you can't replace a fiction that speaks to a universal truth with a lie."

"Was it right to fight?"

"Oh, Simon, it is always the wise and good people that are full of doubts while the fools are always so annoyingly sure of themselves. Yes, it was right."

"Was it right to take a life?"

"Is it right to let injustice reign? –to let the Devil prevail? This ending is really a new beginning. Life is an endless unfoldment towards God, and God waits for his unfoldment in humankind. We just pushed that along a little bit—made that happen sooner than later."

"'I am making everything new.'" Simon quoted The Book of Revelations. Simon asked Preeta to hand him the Bible, which was sitting on a table by his bed. He opened up to Revelations, chapter 21. He read aloud verses 1 to 3: "Then I saw a new heaven and a new Earth, for the first heaven and the first Earth had passed away, and the sea was no more. And I heard a loud voice from the throne saying, 'Behold, the dwelling place of God is with man. He will dwell with them, and they will be his people, and God himself will be with him as their God.'"

"The kingdom of heaven is within you," summarized Preeta.

"And without you," continued Simon.

"May I see the Gospel?" Preeta asked. Simon obliged and Preeta read out loud Revelations 21, verses 4 and 5: "'He will wipe every tear from their eyes. There will be no more death or mourning or crying or pain, for the old order of things has passed away.' And because God is so powerful and righteous, he might even let Satan himself enter the gates of heaven."

"Maybe even Fidelity," suggested Simon.

"No, not Fidelity."

They shared a laugh.

Preeta left him, but her words were comforting, and her visit satiated his ambiguity somewhat. That night, however, while he lay sleeping, a nurse, a die-hard supporter of the former society, entered the room of the weakened Simon and smothered him with a pillow. She was caught by the other nurses and arrested, brought to trial, and subsequently sent to prison for life. Preeta was not willing to take yet another life.

Six months later, Preeta was sitting on a bench in her yard, overlooking her rose garden. She was rubbing her belly like most mothers-to-be do, talking to the baby-to-be, telling the story of its brave father and how he fought for true equality and freedom from tyranny. And she was trying to make sense of her loss, trying to find a simple way of expressing how to sum up the life of her unborn child's father. What could she tell her child to encapsulate what Simon Peter's life was dedicated to? She found a way: "Those were the old ways. We've learned the best way, the only way, is to judge people as individuals."

AUTHOR BIO

Daniel Spiteri is a semi-retired high school mathematics teacher and college instructor of sociology and education, who has published short stories and essays in various magazines over the years. Among those, Daniel published "Disney: Reconciling With a Multicultural Society" and "A Comparative Study of Karl Marx and Adam Smith", the latter published in the American Sociological Journal in 1986 and is still cited today. Mr. Spiteri holds two Bachelor of Arts degrees in Physics and Ethnic Studies from UC Berkeley, and two Master's degrees, Sociology from

Northwestern University, and Education from Cal State East Bay. Daniel was in the Catholic seminary for three years and is a licensed hypnotherapist. Daniel lives in California with his wife. Together they have three children and two grandchildren.

Daniel Spiteri has also written a screenplay to a short film entitled, "In the Name of Man". You may watch it here: https://youtu.be/g0bx-Jo7UgE

Made in the USA
Las Vegas, NV
12 October 2021